PM KAVANAUGH

Dead Inside

Book 2

First edition

Cover art by James, GoOnWrite.com

This book was professionally typeset on Reedsy.
Find out more at reedsy.com

Contents

Acknowledgement

This story sat in my computer, eighty percent finished (well, eighty percent of a decent first draft finished), for over a year while I waited for inspiration, motivation, determination to kick back in. To my delightful surprise, they came in the form of an email from the two women in the first writing group I joined over a decade ago. Both wanted to get back to writing and invited me to join them on regular video calls for sharing and critiquing, because, *hey*, we were in the middle of a pandemic and GoogleMeet/Zoom/Facetime meetings had become a way of life and a way of coping, so why not? Huge thanks to these women—Marcia Tungate and Sharon Henegar—for helping me finish this book AND make it so much better. I also want to thank Meri Cortez for the Spanish translations and California transplant and Anglophile, Lori Rosenwasser, for the British translations. Any mistakes are on me! Special recognition goes to fellow writer KC Klein, who prodded me to get my rights back on Books 1 and 3 of this series so I could realize my dream of self-publishing all three books, with thematic covers and titles, as a proper series. And finally, to Jess Verdi, editor extraordinaire, who made the plot stronger and the emotions deeper. She supplied impressive knowledge, care and tact and actually made the editing process fun. Really! She's awesome.

Chapter 1

"It's time. Get into position. Over."

"Copy that." Anika Washington spoke into her comm device.

Go time.

She inhaled a slow breath to steady her thudding heart. Belgrade's winter air stung her nostrils. Crouched in a corner of the balcony, she stared up at the grayish white sky. The color reminded her of the disgusting synth-milk served at the orphanage where she had grown up.

She lifted into a high squat, making sure to keep her head below the railing. As she stepped forward, her foot slipped on the ice-slick surface. She caught herself from falling.

Focus! No clumsy mistakes. No mistakes period.

She dropped to all fours and crawled forward three meters to her position behind the sniper rifle. Braced on bent elbows, legs stretched out behind her, she was grateful for the insulated unisuit that provided protection from the balcony's cold marble floor. The barrel of the P4 rested in the V of the squat tripod stand. The semi-automatic rifle was a successor to the M4 carbine rifles popular with the United States military in the first half of the twenty-first century. The upgraded weapon performed better, even in extreme weather conditions. This

December day in Serbia qualified. The rifle's tip poked through the hole in the balcony's wall. The advance team had positioned the small opening to provide her the best angle and view to do the job.

She gazed through the scope to sight her target. He squatted low outside the ground floor of the government building opposite the luxury residence where she lay prone on the twentieth floor. That meant her target was 1,084 meters' distance, well within the rifle's maximum range. His dark profile was outlined against the wall of the building. He stood as still as the granite surface beside him. Inside, his team planted explosives.

"On my order, take out the hostile. Over." Anika's team leader, Solomon Nigatu, spoke with practiced authority.

"Copy that." She hoped he didn't hear the strain in her voice. Tension coiled around her neck and shoulders.

This would be her first kill. And unlike the sims she had trained on, next-gen e-games where the hostiles were typically masked and hulked out, this man's face was clearly visible. He looked young—slender, with narrow shoulders and hollow cheeks. Early twenties, she estimated. Her age.

He was actual flesh and blood and bone and muscle. Heart beating. Lungs expanding. Until she fired. One blast, through the temple. Then nothing. Why couldn't she just tranq him? But that wasn't her call. Those weren't her orders. Her orders were to kill.

She had prepared for this moment for so long, first as a new recruit and, more recently, as a Level 1 operative for U.N.I.T, a global counterterrorist organization. She'd thought she was ready to perform in the field. Gianni had said she was ready.

Gianni.

A steel band of anxiety wrapped around her chest. She hadn't seen him since the night of their first mission together. That had been three months ago. Gianni Brambilla was a Level 3 operative, her trainer, and so much more. What had happened to him? Where was he? Not here, not telling her that she had to kill a real live human being.

Her target touched his ear comm and shot upright, stance rigid, on alert.

Through her scope, Anika watched his head swivel to complete a sweep of the area. His head nodded, his lips moved. He was confirming it was safe to exit.

"Take out the hostile. Over," Nigatu said.

Anika firmed her grip on the trigger, inhaled, held her breath. What if the young man hadn't wanted to join the terrorist group, Serbia First?

"Shoot him!" Nigatu's voice sharpened, a knife tip pricking her ear. "Do you copy?"

What if his family had been threatened with death if he refused?

"Takagi, take out Washington's target."

Anika opened her mouth. *No. I've got him. I'll do it.* But the words wouldn't come. And her finger wouldn't move.

From her far right, a single bullet rocketed through the air. The young man's head jerked back from the impact. His body dropped to the ground. Across the courtyard, a similar scenario played out. Another member of her team shot a second watcher. Then more team members took up the positions of the felled terrorists, while others ringed the courtyard's perimeter, out of sight of the building's egress point.

Seconds later, the building's front door handle moved to the open position. Stopped. Takagi, the female operative who had shot Anika's target, pressed the dead man's thumb on the button of his comm wristband to issue the all-clear signal. The door opened. Five hostiles emerged. The dozen-strong U.N.I.T. team erupted from the perimeter, surrounded the group, and forced a quick surrender.

"Washington, report. Over." Nigatu's voice boomed in her ear.

Shitshitshit. What could she say? Weapon jammed? The debriefing machines would discredit her. No clear shot? The advance team would disprove it.

What would happen now? Would she be demoted? Lose her new Level 1 privileges? She had gotten used to more freedom, more sleep, more down time.

"Washington, do you copy?" Nigatu said.

Would her punishment be worse than demotion? Anika's chest tightened. They wouldn't make her leave, would they? Her childhood wound of rejection throbbed deep inside her. She couldn't survive being told she wasn't wanted. Again.

She looked at her right hand, her dominant firing hand. She flexed her fingers, rolled her wrist. In perfect condition. She'd have to change that. Fast.

"I fell. My wrist... it's broken." She whimpered the words. "Over." She waited for the stream of verbal abuse she'd gotten used to in the months of training as a recruit.

"Fuck," Nigatu said. "Copy. Get your ass back to Transport. Over."

"Copy that." Things were clearly different in the field. Or maybe Nigatu was waiting until he could unload on her face-to-face. She disengaged her ear comm. While she had endured countless bone bruises, even a couple of fractures, during her recruit training, she wasn't sure she could keep from crying out in pain from what she was about to do. Still, she could handle the physical pain more than the alternative.

The thin layer of ice on the balcony floor glistened in the early morning light. She took a step. The sole of her boot slid on the smooth surface, then stopped. She'd almost forgotten. *Body cams.* One on her forehead, another behind her right shoulder. Their time recordings would show that she had fallen *after* she had been given the order to shoot. That wouldn't work.

She pulled off her camo head gear and smashed it against the marble. Then she twisted her torso away from the building wall and swung back

4

toward it, whip-fast. Her upper back slammed into the wall. Nothing. She tried again. Harder. It took two more tries before she heard the reassuring *crack* of the camera's glass eye.

She inhaled another deep breath, gritting her teeth. The sting in her throat, the throbbing in her upper back were nothing compared to what was coming.

She ran forward, hit a slight dip, felt her feet slide out from under her. This time, she didn't catch herself, but kept falling and stiffened her arm behind her. She landed hard.

Snap.

Sharp pain shot up her wrist to her shoulder. Then, nausea. Short panting breaths streamed through clenched teeth. The pain was much worse than the bruises and fractures from her hand-to-hand fight training.

Don't pass out. Don't pass out. Don't pass out.

She pressed her right toe against the inside sole of her boot to activate the medical patch. The numbing comfort of a pain blocker flooded her system. In seconds, her wrist quieted. Her stomach continued to churn, and she wondered if she could use it to her advantage. If she vomited in the transport vehicle, maybe she'd garner sympathy. No, strike that. This wasn't the orphanage. This was U.N.I.T., the United Nations Intelligence Trust, the most badass counterterrorism agency on the planet. She'd seem weak as well as incompetent. Standing, she cradled her right arm against her chest, retrieved her weapon, and headed back.

Chapter 2

"How's the wrist?" Nigatu stood outside the door to the debriefing room. His wide-set brown eyes, the same color as his skin, studied her with unblinking intensity.

Anika held up her arm, encased in a flex-cast from hand to elbow. "Great. The medics in Clinic know their stuff. Especially their meds." The combination of pain blockers and soothers had erased any sensation of pain and filled her with calm, all without fogging her head. The bio psych exercises she had practiced during the six-hour journey back to U.N.I.T.'s subterranean complex had helped, too. She felt relaxed, but alert. Ready for the debriefing.

"Yeah, well, the tech in there," he said, jerking his head toward the closed door, "knows her meds, too. If she suspects you're trying to fool the machines, they'll pump you full of shit to make you talk straight." Nigatu's full lips thinned into a disapproving line.

"Don't worry about me," Anika said. "I'll be fine."

"I'm not worried about you." His fist knocked against his thigh in a nervous gesture. "If you fail the debriefing, it won't just be a mark against you. It'll be my ass, too. You're supposed to be the best Level One shooter we have. Don't make me look like a moron for picking you for the mission."

6

"What does a mark mean, anyway?" she asked. "More training? Outside privileges revoked?"

Nigatu snorted. "Marks are serious shit. Get too many, and you're out."

Out? Anxiety fluttered through Anika. *But I just graduated. Just started feeling like I belong here.*

"I won't fail," she said.

On the return flight to New Angeles, in between the bio psych exercises, Anika had replayed the mission in her mind. She'd berated herself over her failure to pull the trigger. Swatted away doubts that she could do this kind of work. Then, she'd committed to redoubling her training on kill sims, and promised herself she would pay more attention to the profiles of the hostiles in future missions so she'd *know* she was taking down bad guys in order to save good guys. She told herself these steps would prevent her from hesitating when the next live kill order came. She willed herself to believe it.

She lifted her chin and held Nigatu's gaze. "I won't make you regret picking me. I'll tell them what they need to hear." *So they won't regret picking me, either.*

"They need to hear what the hell went wrong out there. And they'll be looking for confirmation from the exterior cams."

"Exterior?" The flutter returned, this time like the wings of a panicked bird. She'd only known about the body cams. The ones she had destroyed. Were there really additional cams? Was Nigatu telling the truth, or trying to ensure she did?

"Part of the advance team's prep." Nigatu's eyebrows shot up. "That a problem?"

Anika shrugged to hide the tremor in her shoulders. "No problem."

"Good. Find me in the dining annex later. Let me know how it goes." Nigatu pressed the button on the side wall. The door to the debriefing room hissed open.

"Save me some dessert." She brushed past him. "They're serving chocolate tonight."

* * *

Anika took three steps into the brightly-lit room. A female technician stood beside a high-backed metal chair, the only piece of furniture in the narrow rectangular space. The tech wore a light gray suit that matched the streaks running through her close-cropped brown hair. Her left arm was bent, an e-pad attached to it. She tapped the screen, adjusted the sensors resting on the chair arms, then tapped some more. The room's lights glinted off her rimless glasses as her gaze moved back and forth between the screen and the chair.

"Come in. Sit," she said, not looking up.

The chair's sharp angles dug into Anika's muscles. She forced slow, steady breaths in and out through her nose and focused on a point on the far wall. The tech attached the sensors to her temples, to the pulse points at her left wrist and both ankles, and under her left breast.

This was Anika's second official debriefing, not counting the practice ones during her months of training as a recruit. The first one had been simple and quick, over in twenty minutes. It hadn't involved a technician and sensors, just a machine asking questions and recording answers. Maybe because that mission had gone smoothly. Well, not quite as smoothly as the agency believed.

It had been her first mission, the one that would allow her to graduate from recruit to Level 1 status. It had taken place at the gala to celebrate the opening of the North Korean embassy in Washington, D.C. While she'd succeeded in her assignment to obtain a nano disc from the safe in the ambassador's study, the prototype device inside her shoe that unlocked the safe had malfunctioned and triggered the alarm. Imprisoned in the study by titanium bars, she had faced certain capture—perhaps death—by the embassy guards. If Gianni hadn't created a diversion to help her escape...

Gianni, where are you?

"Let's begin," the tech said. "State your name, tracking ID, rank."

"Anika Washington. Kilo-bravo-foxtrot-one-seven-two-nine-five. Level One operative."

A corner of the tech's mouth turned down. She adjusted the sensor on Anika's left wrist and tapped her screen once. "State your U.N.I.T. and location."

"U.N.I.T. six-zero-five. New Angeles."

"Where were you recruited from?"

"A federal orphanage outside of Washington, D.C." *More like rescued from there*, Anika thought.

The tech nodded a fraction, apparently satisfied with the equipment. "Why didn't you shoot the target?"

Anika's throat constricted, cutting off her next inhale. The easy questions were over. "I...couldn't," she said.

"Explain."

Anika's next words had to be chosen with care. She had to convince herself so her vital signs would convince the sensors. She closed her eyes and visualized herself back on the balcony, lying down, ready to shoot the target.

No, back up, she thought. *Start earlier.*

She was in a corner of the balcony. Crouched against the side wall, the marble structure solid against her back. Milk-colored sky. "I heard the order to get ready. Acknowledged it, then started to move into position." She remembered lifting up from her crouch, stepping forward, starting to fall. "The balcony floor was covered in ice." In her mind, she didn't catch herself. She fell. In the debriefing room, she winced as she relived the actual fall. The sharp crack of bone, the hot pain up her arm. "I slipped. Landed on my wrist. Heard it break."

"Why didn't you tell your team lead?"

"I thought I could still shoot. Use my non-dominant hand. The way we were taught during training." A mix of lie and truth. "But I..." Anika remembered the paralysis that gripped her after receiving the order to shoot. "I couldn't move." *True.*

A faint tapping on the e-pad came from behind her.

She opened her eyes. Refocused on a distant point. Re-steadied her breath. She didn't try to fill the quiet. Didn't try to over explain. The less said, the better. She hoped.

"How do you feel now?"

"Fine. The medics fixed me up and—"

"Not physically." The tech cut her off. "What is your emotional state?"

The question startled her. She hadn't been asked that in her prior debriefing. What was the right answer now? What should she feel?

"Uncertainty," she said.

"Continue."

"I'm wondering what will happen to me since I...was unable to complete the mission. Will I be disciplined? Or..." Despite her best efforts, Anika's breath faltered and her heart quickened. The machines had to be registering her distress. "Or told to leave." She swallowed. "I feel..." *Terror, dread.* "Anxious."

"Anything else?"

What should a committed operative feel? Frustration at her own incompetence? Remorse at letting the agency down?

She closed her eyes and thought of the one person who could inspire feelings strong enough to convince the machines she was telling the truth. She recalled their last minutes together on the night of her first mission. The gleam of moonlight on his dark-blond hair, the desire in his brown eyes, warm lips on hers when they kissed for the first time.

Where are you? Why haven't you come back?

"I need a spoken answer," the tech prodded.

Anika blew out a breath. "I'm frustrated."

"Is that everything? I need to submit a full report."

She should have said *yes* to him that night. *Yes* to his invitation for coffee at the café that reminded him of home. *Yes* to a romantic relationship.

Even though they both knew it was dangerous. It risked breaking an agency rule. U.N.I.T. didn't permit any behavior that might jeopardize mission performance. That included forming strong attachments inside or outside the agency. It especially included romantic relationships between operatives. The instructors had made that very clear in the first weeks of training.

Gianni had told her that as long as they both maintained mission proficiency, they could follow the agency's rule *and* pursue a relationship. He had said it was worth the risk. *She* was worth the risk. His admission had both scared and thrilled her. Mostly thrilled.

Then he had told her to think about it and give him an answer when she was ready. She should have said *yes* right then. Instead, she stayed silent as he boarded the jet plane and flew off on a new mission. Only when he was in the air, out of earshot, had she whispered her acceptance. He didn't know how much she wanted him, how much she missed him. Her shoulders drooped. "I feel regret."

The tech appeared at Anika's side and removed the sensors. "You can go."

Anika licked her dry lips. "How did I do?"

"I'll provide the results to Second," she said, referring to the female officer who was second-in-command at U.N.I.T. 605. "Remain on premise until you receive further instructions."

Chapter 3

Anika awoke the next morning in a private room reserved for Level 1 operatives. The first thing she saw was her friend, Mari Barnes, another newly-graduated operative, sitting on the floor at the foot of her bed. Her curly hair was bunched in a knot atop her head.

Anika pressed her fingertips against her closed eyes, gritty from a restless night of troubling dreams. "I feel like droid crap," she said.

Mari didn't respond. With her back against the bedframe, arms wrapped tight around bent knees, she stared at the blank wall in front of her.

Anika rolled over on her side. "You all right?"

Mari turned her head. Her blue eyes were wide and unblinking. "I have a new mission." Mari's words came out in a hoarse whisper.

Anika sat up. "Oka-a-ay. Is that bad?" Her mind felt sluggish. "You did fine on your first mission. Graduated to Level One, like me. So, what's the problem?"

"You know I can't tell you." Mari hung her head. "You're not part of the team."

"I know that." Anika's voice sharpened in irritation. She was so tired from tossing and turning for the past eight hours. Mari curled into herself even more. The gesture slap-stung Anika. She took a breath and smoothed the edge from her voice. "Don't give me any details. Just tell me what's got you spooked."

"Unless..." Mari's eyebrows lifted and her face regained some color. "Can you ask to be assigned to it? I'd feel so much better if you were on it, too."

Anika counted to three before responding. "I don't think they'll assign me to any missions with this." She held up her wrist, still in the flex-cast.

Her injury hadn't caused her restlessness. Neither had the debriefing results. The previous night, Nigatu had found her at the dessert bar. She'd been trying to decide between two options—as a new Level 1, she still had to adhere to the agency's nutrition requirements. The cherry-flavored gel cup would only cost her a single day's credit of sugar and fat, whereas the twelve-layer chocolate skyscraper would use up her dessert credits for the rest of the month. But after the day she'd had, maybe it was worth it.

"Congratulations," Nigatu had said. "You passed the debriefing. Starting tomorrow, report in for more arms training. Left-handed shooting, until you're as proficient as your dominant hand."

A cool breeze of relief rushed through her. She ordered the chocolate skyscraper.

Given the good news, she'd thought she would sleep like a baby. Instead, her dreams had been filled with images of the terrorist, mixed with ones of Gianni gazing into her eyes, waiting for her answer. Paralysis gripped her as she tried to move her trigger finger, as she tried to form words. More than once, she had shot upright in bed, squeezing an imaginary trigger and crying out *yes*.

"I have to rappel off a thirty-story building," Mari said, shuddering. "During the mission."

"You're still afraid of heights?" Anika asked. "Even with all the bio psych training?"

Mari nodded. "What am I going to do?"

"Same as me." Anika swung her feet to the floor and stood up. Reaching down, she grabbed Mari's arm, and pulled her to standing. "Hit the showers, then the dining annex, then the training facility, where we're going to train until you can rappel and I can shoot left-handed like it's encoded into our DNA."

* * *

Forty-seven minutes later, Anika and Mari stood at the base of the rappelling wall, harnesses and ropes in their gloved hands. Back here, they could barely hear the sounds of other operatives and recruits training in the forward areas—running laps on the gyro-tracks, firing practice rounds in the target chambers, engaging in hand-to-hand fighting.

Mari looked up at the wall that ran eleven stories high. "I'm going to be sick."

"I told you not to eat that third pancake," Anika said. "Didn't that use up all your carb credits for the week?"

"Worth it." Marie swallowed. "I eat when I'm nervous."

"You'll be fine. We'll start slow with a six-meter rappel. Okay?"

"Three-meter."

"That's not a rappel. That's a jump-and-roll," Anika said. "Six meters."

Mari nodded, a sheen of sweat coating her pale skin.

They slipped on their harnesses, attached the ropes, and entered the auto-lift. When they stopped at the six-meter mark, Mari didn't move. She was as still as she had been that morning at the foot of Anika's bed.

Anika grabbed her friend by the shoulders. "You can do this. Take it one step at a time. Keep breathing. And whatever you do, don't look down."

Moving as if sludge had replaced the blood in her veins, Mari exited the lift onto the ledge that ran the width of the wall. Anika followed. Seven steps out, they turned to face the wall, their backs to the open expanse behind them.

Anika could hear the *clickclickclick* of Mari's teeth. "Brace your legs against the ledge and lean back." She watched Mari adopt the proper pre-release stance. "On the count of three. One, two..." She reached for the green button on her gear. Stopped. Mari had gone still again. "Three!" She punched her and Mari's release buttons at the same time.

"Noooo!" Mari cried.

"Pump your legs," Anika yelled as they dropped. "Lean forward more." The ground below loomed closer.

Within seconds, they touched down.

Anika turned to face her friend, whose face had lost some of its pallor. "See? Piece of ca—"

Mari's fist shot out and landed in Anika's gut. Despite her pretty features and slender frame, she packed a mean punch. "Why did you hit my release button?" Mari roared. "I wasn't ready."

Anika took a few deep breaths, fighting for control of her stomach—and her anger. "Your teeth have stopped chattering. So..." She sucked in another breath. "You're welcome. Now that you're pissed off instead of scared, we'll go again. Twelve meters."

Mari scowled and crossed her arms.

"And this time," Anika said, keeping her voice even, "we'll change the scenario. More like a real mission. We'll do a double rappel. I'll pretend to be a hostile whom you've been ordered to capture for interrogation."

A gleam appeared in Mari's eye. "If that's the case, shouldn't you be unconscious because you've resisted and I've had to kick your ass into submission?"

"Good point." Anika dropped to the ground and lay still, playing her part. She trusted that her friend had exorcised her anger with that one punch. And she hoped that the effort of having to drag her body into the lift, attach their harnesses, and maneuver them both onto the ledge would keep Mari from thinking too much about the height of the next rappel.

The next minutes were filled with Mari's grunts and curses as she executed a clean double rappel. When they landed back at the base of the wall, Anika opened her eyes and clapped Mari on the shoulder. "Great job."

Mari bent forward and vomited the remains of her pancake breakfast onto the floor.

Anika disengaged her harness from Mari's and walked over to a wall panel. She keyed in a request for a service droid, then grabbed a piece of plastic tubing positioned at waist height along the wall. Flipping open one end of the tube, she brought it to her mouth and gulped down cucumber-flavored water. "Clean-up droid is coming," she said. "Want some?" She held out the tube of water.

Mari nodded and took a few sips. "Ugh, I hate cucumber. Why can't they flavor this stuff with cherry or something decent?"

After the droid had wiped up the vomit and scented the air with the fresh smell of a spring morning, Anika asked, "Ready to go again?"

Mari sighed and gave a weak smile. "Sure, what the hell. Until it's encoded in our DNA, right?"

"Right."

When they had completed two more rappels, each one progressively higher, Anika decided she could leave her friend to practice on her own. She removed her handheld from her sleeve pocket and took a picture of Mari, cheeks rosy, eyes bright. She turned the screen to her friend. "See? Proof you're still alive."

"I guess." Mari shrugged. "I wish I weren't so afraid."

"Remember what they told us in our recruit days. Sometimes, the fear won't go away. So you have to do it—"

"Afraid." Mari grimaced. "I hate that Zen crap."

Anika laughed. "I've got to take off." She stepped out of her harness and wiped the sweat off her face. "You keep at it, okay?"

"You're leaving?" Mari's color dimmed.

"I need to hit the target chamber and practice shooting with my left hand, or Nigatu will have my ass."

"Want some company?" Mari asked. "I could use some left-handed target practice myself. Then we could do more rappelling this afternoon." Mari started to remove her harness, but Anika stopped her.

"I have PT this afternoon." Anika grimaced. "With the EO machine," she added, referring to the electro-osteo stimulator that accelerated bone recovery. She had endured many sessions during her ten months as a recruit. Painful, but effective.

"Double ugh," Mari said.

"Yeah, well, that'll teach me to stop being so clumsy when I'm in the field."

"Is that really why you fell?" Mari asked.

Guilt squeezed Anika's chest. She wanted to tell the truth, but she was afraid. For herself and her friend. If Mari were ever asked, Anika didn't want her to have to lie.

"You were never clumsy during recruit training," Mari added.

The pressure in Anika's chest increased. Anxiety overrode guilt. Were people questioning her version of what had happened? Had Mari heard something? But she had passed the debriefing test. Nigatu had confirmed it.

Anika shrugged. "It's different in the field. You know that."

"Yeah, I guess," Mari said, turning her attention back to her gear. "Want to meet up for dinner?"

"Sure. That would be great." The tightness in Anika's chest eased.

"And Mari?" Her friend looked up, eyebrows raised. "No second helpings at lunch, okay?"

Mari rolled her eyes. "Copy that!"

Chapter 4

Anika slid her food tray onto a table for two in a corner of the dining annex. The gel-carpeted floor and sound-absorbent walls muted the noises in the room. The relative quiet was a welcome change from the large, noisy hall where she and the other recruits used to eat.

She stared at her plate of angel hair pasta with tomato cream sauce and a side of sourdough bread soaked in herb-scented olive oil. *Comfort food.* She should have skipped the bread, or the oil, or both. They used up most of her carb and fat credits for the week. At this rate, she'd be limited to vegetable nuggets with protein additives for the next several days.

She rested her sore wrist on the table. It still ached from the final round with the EO machine. She twirled strands of the thin silky noodles around her fork. *Food from Gianni's native country.* The unbidden thought streaked through her mind and she dropped the fork. *Stop it! Stop thinking about him.*

She stabbed at the pasta again, lifted up a mound of it, and shoved it into her mouth. Creamy warmth slid down her throat. The quality of the food was also a welcome change from the glop served to recruits. Even with the nutritional restrictions.

A view would be nice, she thought, staring at the blank wall ahead of her. But the building didn't include windows to the outside. What would be the point? The only things to see outside the walls of the subterranean complex were layers of rock and dirt. And a window-sized hologram of the ocean at sunset or a mountain vista would probably be considered too much of a distraction from the tough-minded workings of the agency.

She reached for the bread and pulled off a chunk. *Concentrate on your advanced training, even if he's not here to supervise it, like he promised. And don't screw up again. Do—*

"Guess what?" Mari plopped down into the chair opposite Anika. Her hands fisted in front of her mouth as if she was trying to hold back a secret. Before Anika could speak, Mari blurted out, "My mission's been called off!" Her eyes sparkled, twin blue-colored diamonds. "Isn't that great?"

"Mari." Anika brought her fingers to her lips in a "stop talking" gesture. Her gaze swept the area around them. None of the operatives seated nearby glanced their way. They were engaged in their own conversations or engrossed with their handhelds. Still, the steady red light on three security cams told Anika the room was being monitored. "We're not alone, you know."

"Who cares?" Mari jiggled in her seat. "I'm not saying anything about the mission itself. Just that it's been canceled. I got word after lunch. I wanted to tell you right away, but the PT goons wouldn't let me in to see you."

Anika eyebrows drew together and her lips twisted in confusion. "Canceled or postponed?"

Mari shrugged. "Canceled. For now. That's good enough for me. I'm going to grab a tray." She eyed Anika's plate. "That looks credit-busting, by the way. Be right back." She jumped up and hurried over to the auto-serve station.

"How did the rappelling go this afternoon?" Anika asked when Mari returned with a tray of steak and potatoes smothered in gravy. "What was your longest descent?"

Mari cut into her meat and speared a bite. "Want a taste?" She extended her fork.

Anika shook her head and leaned back. Mari dropped her gaze. "Tell me you practiced. We had a deal."

"Easy for you to say." Mari continued to stare at her plate. "You're not afraid of anything."

"That's not true," Anika said.

"Oh, yeah?" Mari's gaze shot up. The sparkle in her eyes had grown hotter, like the diamonds had been thrown into a fire. "Name one."

Anika bit down on her lip. Even if there'd been no security cams, she didn't know how much she should reveal to her friend. "I'm afraid... " She lowered her voice. "I'm afraid of screwing up my next mission and getting kicked out of here." Even if it wasn't the whole story, the statement was true. And similar to what she had said in the debriefing.

"Well, that's not going to happen." The fire in Mari's gaze dampened and she took a bite of food. "Not to our class's top recruit, who graduated two months before everyone else."

"Everyone except Jett," Anika whispered. Jett Silva had been assigned the North Korean embassy mission ahead of Anika. But she had been killed in the middle of it and Anika had been ordered to step in as her replacement.

"Jett didn't graduate. She didn't complete the mission. You did. And you haven't screwed up since."

Anika held up her broken wrist. "What do you call this?"

"Wardrobe screw-up," Mari said. "Your boots should have been treated with an anti-slip coating, or something."

"I wish I had thought of that for the debriefing," Anika said.

"It's not like you missed your target," Mari continued. "You didn't get a chance to take your shot."

Anika's stomach clenched. If only her friend were right.

"Don't be mad at me for not practicing," Mari said, mistaking Anika's expression as disapproval instead of self-reproach. "Please? I couldn't make myself do it."

Affection for her friend unfurled in Anika. Her stomach unclenched and her mouth relaxed. "I'm not mad." She squeezed Mari's hand in reassurance. She hadn't felt friendship toward anyone in a long time. Not since Skye and Nadia, close friends of hers in the orphanage. Until they were both adopted and joined their new families, leaving Anika behind. She had made up her mind that it was less painful to avoid getting close to anyone after that. But now that she and Mari both belonged at U.N.I.T., had both been chosen as recruits, had both graduated, they wouldn't leave each other behind. "It's just that I want you to kick ass in here. So we can both stay."

"Tomorrow." Mari took in a deep breath. "Back to the wall. I promise." She looked down at her empty plate, then over at Anika's. "You going to finish that?" she asked, eyeing the swirls of pasta.

"Yes!" Anika laughed. "Besides, you know sharing's against the rules. If you're still hungry, go get your own."

While Mari was gone, Anika pushed the noodles around on her plate. Her plan to practice away her fear of a live kill seemed to be working. During her session in the target chamber, she had programmed scenarios that mimicked yesterday's mission to try and overcome her feelings of resistance. When the order to shoot had come through her ear comm, she had pulled the trigger without hesitation. Still, she wondered—and worried—if her willingness to fire was because she'd known, deep inside, the kill wasn't real.

"I decided to move onto dessert." Mari set down two plates loaded with colorful confections.

"None for me, thanks," Anika said.

"These aren't for you!" Mari replied, taking a bite out of a chocolate-

and-pink layer cake. "What's wrong, though? I've never seen you pass up dessert, especially chocolate. Don't tell me you've used up all your sugar and fat credits."

She had, but that wasn't the only reason she'd turned down Mari's offer. She had too much on her mind. "Can I ask you something?"

"Sure." A small puff of powdered sugar escaped through Mari's lips. "Sorry." She waved away the sugary motes.

"Without giving away any details," Anika said, still mindful of the electronic eyes and ears stationed around the room, "have any of your missions required a live kill?"

Mari swallowed. "Yeah, both of them."

"How did you..." Anika took a breath and decided on another approach. "Did it feel different than in our sims workshops?"

"I guess." Mari shrugged. "Like you said, it's different in the field." She picked up her second dessert, a round marble of dark chocolate. "Sure you don't want some?"

Anika shook her head. Her appetite had vanished. How could her friend be so casual about killing someone? "How did it feel? After you fired?"

"I thought it might bother me, you know?" Mari's eyebrows quirked upward. "So I pretended the target was a sick-ass child abuser. Like my father and my uncle." Her cheeks flushed an angry red as she spit out the last words. "As soon as I thought of that, I pulled the trigger." Mari pushed away the unfinished desserts. "Guess my eyes were bigger than my stomach."

"Sorry if I..." Anika shook her head. "I shouldn't have asked."

"What about you?"

"I...haven't done one. Yet."

"Hmm." Mari studied Anika, who tensed under her friend's watchful gaze. *Don't ask. Please don't ask.* "Well, you will. Just like I'm going to execute a perfect rappel, right?"

Anika forced a smile. "Damn right."

Chapter 5

The flashing light on Anika's handheld indicated a new message. "I'm here. U coming?" The photo showed Mari standing next to the rappelling wall, already geared up. Time received: 0450 hours.

Anika groaned. "Now you're all fired up about practicing?" she said to the empty room. Her voice was a sleep-deprived rasp. "OMW," she typed, followed by a vulgar hand gesture. On second thought, she deleted the gesture, hit send, and eased herself out of bed.

As a Level 1, she had her own apartment outside U.N.I.T, and could usually sleep in an extra hour. But she had promised to meet Mari back at the rappelling walls for a few runs before her own weapons practice, so she'd slept on premise again last night.

She felt heavy-eyed and sore-muscled—the discomforts reminded her of recruit training. She didn't miss those days. After a quick shower with a freezing-cold finish to chase away the remnants of sleep, she dressed and headed out.

She rounded the final turn of the corridor leading to the training facility, then stopped, immobilized with surprise. Was she still asleep? She blinked twice. Half a dozen operatives, in assault gear, were grouped together at the facility's entrance. Along the side wall, two medics checked the controls on idling gurneys and inspected their medical field kits. Standing at the head of the assault team, his dark blond hair slicked back into a low tail, was the man Anika had spent a restless night dreaming about.

Conflicting emotions, like jabs in a fistfight, pummeled her. Joy that he was back, relief that he was safe, anger that he hadn't contacted her. *Where have you been?* she wanted to shout. *When did you get back? Why didn't you come find me?*

But her emotions—and her questions—would have to wait until they were alone.

She dashed forward.

As she drew close to the group, Gianni's gaze met hers. Some emotion shimmered in his chocolate brown eyes. Desire? Remorse? It vanished before she could decide. In its place, a look of intense focus etched lines into the corners of his eyes and mouth.

"What's...hap...pening?" Her breath erupted in bursts. And not because of the running.

"Two hostiles from the Belgrade mission escaped the interrogation quarters," Gianni said. "They took out the guards, stole weapons. We tracked them to the training facility."

Anxiety spiked inside her. "Mari's in there. We're supposed to meet at the rappelling walls. She sent me a message a few minutes ago."

Gianni checked his handheld. "I see one heat signature near the walls."

"It must be her. I want to go in." Gianni glanced at her still-casted wrist. "I've been training with my left-hand," she said. "I can help." His gaze returned to her face. No warmth there. Only a cool appraisal. Anika stiffened, her spine titanium alloy. "You promised advanced training, remember?" she said, referring to the last time they had seen each other. They had been standing on the tarmac near the evac plane after the North Korean embassy mission. "This is advanced."

26

That got a reaction from him. A spark of shared memory flickered in his eyes.

He turned to the sharp-featured female operative on his right. She was about Anika's height and build. Anika recognized her from the Belgrade mission—it was Yosh Takagi. Hers was the shot that had killed the hostile when Anika hesitated.

"Takagi, stand down," Gianni said. "Give Anika your gear and weapon."

Takagi's dark eyes narrowed. "I covered for her in Belgrade. Took out her target when she didn't."

"You didn't *cover* for me," Anika fired back. "I fell and broke my wrist."

Takagi snorted in reply.

"I gave you an order, Takagi." Gianni's voice was low and dangerous, a storm cloud hovering overhead.

Takagi stepped back. "Yes, sir." She stripped off her body armor and tossed it at Anika, who instinctively caught it with her dominant hand.

She felt the catch all the way up to her shoulder. Blocking out the pain, she took the laser and ear comm from Takagi. The dismissed operative strode off, her body rigid with controlled fury. Anika ran the checks on the weapon to confirm it was fully charged. She donned the protective gear, gripped the laser in her left hand, and disengaged the safety.

"Except for Mari in the rappelling section, all bodies are clustered together in one of the small training rooms along the eastern wall," Gianni said to the assembled group. "Most likely, the hostiles have corralled the operatives who were inside and are holding them as hostages, waiting for an assault. Let's give it to them. Those of you with lasers, set them to maximum force."

"Not stun?" Anika asked.

"We're not risking our people's lives. Understood?" His gaze was as hard as his words.

Anika adjusted the laser's setting.

"Say it," Gianni said.

His words scraped like a turbo sander. "Understood."

"We'll handle the hostiles and the hostages," he told her. "You go to the rappelling walls. Find Mari and wait there until I give the all-clear."

Anika gave a final tug to her body armor and focused on the doors of the facility. "Yes, sir."

"One more thing." Gianni stepped closer to her, his voice low. "If you get a chance to fire, don't hesitate. Take the shot."

Anika's eyebrows drew together. Why was he saying this? Did he suspect the truth of what had happened in Belgrade? Regardless of what he suspected, resolve steeled her. She was determined to save Mari, whatever it took.

She firmed her grip on the laser. "I will."

Gianni disengaged the locks to the facility. "Move out."

The team surged forward and turned right as soon as it entered the hangar-like room. Typically abuzz with the breaths, punches, thumps, and thuds of bodies and exercise equipment, the space was now eerily quiet and empty—except for one body in workout gear that lay prone on the ground, facedown, a dark pool of blood spreading out from his chest. The medics glided a gurney toward him. Anika prayed they weren't too late, but didn't stay to find out. She had to find Mari. Crouching low, out of sight of the acrylic walls that fronted the series of small training rooms on the other side of the vast space, she broke away to the left, and headed for the far wall.

When she had cleared the open space, she straightened and ran full speed past the target chambers toward the back of the facility and the rappelling walls. As she neared the place where she and Mari had been practicing yesterday, her pulse kicked up a notch. A rappelling rope lay in a jumbled heap at the base of the wall. No sign of her friend. She did a visual sweep of the area. Gianni had said he saw movement here, but that was minutes ago. Maybe Mari had been discovered and herded in with the other hostages.

She engaged her ear comm and turned toward the front of the facility. "Mari's not here. Should I head back? Do you copy?"

No answer.

That's when she heard it. A muffled squeak. From behind her, near the auto-lift in the corner. She spun back, laser pointing in the direction of the sound.

In the auto-lift's doorway stood her friend. Behind her, a foot taller and twenty pounds heavier, was a man. Anika recognized him as one of the hostiles captured in Belgrade. The man's hands gripped Mari's ponytail, pulling her head back. The other held a syringe against the side of her neck.

Gianni had said there was only one heat signature back here. Apparently, he'd been wrong.

Anika winced at her friend's swollen eye and split lip. Mari's right shoulder drooped unnaturally. At least she had put up a fight.

The man bore his own signs of abuse. But most of his bruises, an ugly mix of black, purple, and green, looked old. *Interrogation*, Anika thought.

Don't hesitate, Gianni had said. *Take the shot.* But she didn't have a clear shot, not with Mari in the way.

"Let her go," Anika said, voice firm, left arm steady. "We've breached the facility and are freeing the others now. It's over." She hadn't heard any sounds coming from the front of the facility. Had the other hostiles surrendered? Given up without a fight?

"Give me code to auto-lift," the man said in broken English. "Your friend won't tell me. If you don't, I'll pump syringe into her. It's full of synthetic used to make me talk."

From this distance, Anika couldn't tell if the syringe was full or empty. If full, that large a dose could likely kill a woman Mari's size.

Even if empty, air injected directly into her jugular vein could cause an embolism resulting in death by stroke or cardiac arrest.

"Why do you need the auto-lift?" Anika asked.

"Emergency exit at top."

Anika shook her head. "There is no exit."

"Don't lie. I overheard guards talking. How they use it when they want to leave this shithole for few hours."

Was there an exit? Anika had never heard of one. But then, she didn't know everything about this place. "I'm telling you, there's no exit. The only way out of this place is through the front door. And you'll never get there alive."

The hostile released Mari's hair and clamped his forearm around her neck. Squeezed. A breath wheezed from Mari's mouth and the color seeped from her face.

Anika's stomach roiled, as if a street cat was trying to claw its way out. *I don't want to shoot you. But I will, if that's the only way to save Mari.*

"Okay, okay," she said, still pointing her laser. *Stall.* "I'll give you the code. But it only works with print recognition. You'll need this." She pointed her free thumb up in the air.

The man relaxed his hold and Mari gasped in and out. "I'll use her thumb."

Mari started making one-handed signals, out of sight of the man's line of vision.

Anika couldn't drop her gaze and study the signals without calling attention to them. Limited to only her peripheral vision, she struggled to decipher what Mari was trying to tell her.

"She's only a recruit," Anika said. "You need the print of a higher level operative. Like me." Not true, but he didn't know that. "Let her go. I'll ride up with you and input the code. If you're right, and there's an exit door, it will be coded, too."

She needed to buy time. *Once we get to the top,* she thought, *and he sees for himself there's no exit, then ride back down, Gianni will be here.* Even though she hadn't heard anything through her comm device, he had to be tracking what was happening back here. He had to be.

The man backed into the auto-lift. He dragged Mari with him. As they moved farther away from her, Anika could see Mari's signals better, but the angle of her friend's hand still made them hard to interpret. Thumb and forefinger moving toward each other? Fist opening to splayed fingers? Two signals. Over and over.

"Okay, we all ride up together," the man said. "And if there's no exit, I make one."

Make an exit? How?

Mari signed faster. Thumb and forefinger. Fist and splayed fingers.

Her meaning suddenly became clear. Mini-grenade. The hostile had one. But how? They were secured in munitions lockers, nowhere near the interrogation rooms. Unless they'd been used as part of a negotiating tactic?

Gianni had been right. She had to take the hostile out. The cat in her stomach was now a frantic jumble of claws and teeth.

Anika trained her gaze on the man's upper chest, where the "V" neckline of his T-shirt came to a point. Though uncomfortably close to the top of Mari's head, it was a decent-sized target area. She took two steps closer, waiting for the right moment. With her other hand, she crossed her second finger over her forefinger and, with tiny movements, flicked them left and right. Twice. She hoped Mari understood. *Get ready.*

"Come," the hostile said. "Get in."

Mari's first two fingers extended, thumb pointing out. Her head dipped. Her body sagged. She dropped her thumb and swept her hand forward. *Shoot!*

Anika fired. The laser hit the man's forehead above his right eye. Not where she had intended, but it did the job. His arms jerked sideways and

Mari scrambled free. His body fell back against the lift wall and slumped to the floor.

Anika stared at his face, skin paling beneath his dark complexion, jaw slackening, eyes unstaring. It would haunt her dreams. Her first live kill.

Mari walked toward her.

"You okay?" Anika asked.

Mari nodded, the color beginning to return to her face. "You?"

Anika bent forward, resting her hands on her knees, and gulped in some deep breaths. "Good hand signaling. Sorry it took me so long to figure out."

"Good shot," Mari said.

"Excellent shot." Gianni's voice came from behind her.

Anika spun around. He stood two meters away, a team member on either side.

"I was aiming for his upper chest," Anika admitted.

"My assessment stands," Gianni replied. "You did well." He glanced at Mari. "You both did."

"He caught me after my first rappel," Mari said. "I was so focused on landing I didn't see him until he was on me."

Anika looked at Gianni. "I thought your handheld showed only one heat signature back here."

"If the hostile had a tight hold on Mari, they would read as one." He directed his attention to Mari. "How are your injuries?"

"Nothing the medics in Clinic can't fix."

"Good. Report there. Your mission that was canceled is back on. Confirm when you'll be field ready."

Anika watched her friend's face pale again.

"I'd like to join the mission," Anika said.

"You're being assigned to a different one," Gianni replied.

Anika brows lifted. "I am? When?"

"You'll be briefed tomorrow. Report in at oh-six-hundred-hours."
Gianni turned his gaze to Mari. "You should go now. Get checked out."

"I'll come find you later," Anika said.

Mari nodded, her good eye clouded with worry, and walked away.

One of the medics appeared with a gurney. The team members who had accompanied Gianni moved toward the body.

"Be careful," Anika said. "He's carrying a mini-grenade."

They found the explosive in the man's pant pocket. A dark plum-shaped object of destruction. His body was lifted onto the gurney and the group moved off, toward the front of the facility.

Anika watched them go. A tiny alarm of suspicion vibrated inside her. "How did he get his hands on a mini-grenade? It doesn't make sense." She looked at Gianni.

His gaze was neutral, giving nothing away.

Which raised her suspicions even more.

Chapter 6

"What happened with the others?" Anika asked.

"The operatives are all fine," Gianni replied. "The hostiles surrendered."

"Without a fight?"

"They have families in Novi Sad. We promised not to harm them, if they gave themselves up."

"I wish I had known that about my hostile. Maybe he would have given up, too."

"But then you wouldn't have shot him."

The vibration intensified. Something wasn't right. "You sound as if that would've been a *bad* thing."

"You would have avoided your first live kill. Again."

"That's what this was about?" Her hands clenched into fists as she realized what he was saying. "This whole thing was a set-up? You let the hostiles out on *purpose*? To make me kill someone?"

"You've now crossed that line, as every operative must. The next time you're in the field, and you're given an order to shoot, you won't hesitate." His voice was flat, devoid of emotion.

"You risked everyone's life. Mari's, the other operatives', mine."

"That is the kind of life we all live in here."

"He had a *grenade*, Gianni." Something flickered in his eyes. She sensed he was holding something back. "It wasn't live, was it?" she realized aloud.

"He thought it was."

"And the syringe?"

"Saline solution."

Anika gave a sharp exhale. The deception, and her inability to see through it, had landed a sucker punch to the gut.

"Today wasn't just about you," Gianni continued. "It was a drill. A test. For you, for Mari, for the others. You all passed."

"What about the operative lying on the floor in his own blood?"

"He'll live," Gianni said. "But not for long, if his instincts or his skills for surviving an assault don't improve."

"What's wrong with you?" she burst out. Where was the man who had held her in his arms, kissed her, told her he wanted *more* from her? "You're so... how can you not care?"

His gaze cut right, then left, taking in the area around them.

Shit, Anika thought. *Surveillance cams.*

She knew better than to try and have this kind of conversation out in the open. Annoyance at her rookie mistake clashed with anger at Gianni. She half expected him to walk away.

Instead, he strode to the northern outer wall of the auto-lift and gestured for her to follow. When she came within earshot, he said, "Camera dead spot."

She nodded in understanding. He couldn't tell her where he had been, what he had been doing, so she wouldn't waste time asking. "When did you get back?"

"Last night."

"Why didn't you let me know?"

"There was no time. I had to finish my debriefing, then review the Belgrade mission report, prepare my assessment, and plan today's drill."

Her emotions cooled, ice chips tossed on a hot sidewalk. In their place, trepidation. "Your assessment?"

"I'm still the senior officer in charge of your training."

"What did you conclude?"

"The exterior cameras suggested your fall took place *after* you received the order to fire."

Anika's breath stopped in her throat. She refused to look at him, afraid he would see the truth in her eyes.

"However, there were gaps in the recording," Gianni said. "I was forced to rely on your answers and the sensor readings."

When the silence between them had stretched to a painful length, Anika cleared her throat. "I trust they were satisfactory."

"Barely."

She made herself look at him then. "What does that mean?"

"It means no disciplinary action. You'll continue your advanced training. The team leader, Nigatu, made a bad judgment call. He shouldn't have tried to use you for a live kill. He was overly influenced by your firing proficiency, but failed to consider your psychological profile."

"My... profile? Does it say I can't shoot a live target?" Fear rolled through her, setting off tremors. *How will I survive in here?*

"You need the proper motivation. Today, you killed one hostile to save one operative. In the field, you typically will kill one to save many. Fellow operatives, civilians, often both. Remember that the next time."

Next time. There would always be a next time. The trembling stopped, replaced by a heavy resignation. Saving the world from those who sought to destroy it would sometimes require an extreme act. A live kill. What else had she expected when she joined a counterterrorist organization?

"Is that all?" she asked.

"One more thing."

"What is it?"

"You need to debrief on what happened here. If asked, don't acknowledge hesitating when you first encountered the hostile. Say you were angling for a better shot."

"I *was* angling for a better shot. So I wouldn't accidentally hit Mari."

"Fair enough. You should add to that. Say you thought you could spare the hostile. Take him down with a non-lethal shot."

"Your order was to kill."

"My order was to set your weapon to maximum force. Which you did."

"In order to kill. To save our own."

"Tell them you thought you could save both. Keep the hostile alive for a possible future trade. That demonstrates bigger picture thinking. Shows progress in your training. And it proves commitment to U.N.I.T. and what we stand for."

"Taking out bad guys?" Sarcasm threaded through her words. Nothing in Gianni's eyes or words suggested she was anything to him but an operative in need of more training. Anger returned with a vengeance, sizzling through her. "Did you even mean what you said to me that night on the tarmac? About wanting me, wanting *us*? Or was that just motivation...to strengthen my *commitment*?"

His gaze lashed like a whip. "I meant it."

Good. She had forced a momentary connection, even if it was full of anger.

"Then why didn't I hear from you?" The words shot out, unfiltered. "Three months and not a word. I know you couldn't say where you were, what your mission was. But you could at least have found a way to tell me you were still alive, still coming back."

Gianni glanced away for a moment and studied the wall over her head. He reached up and adjusted a silver chain around his neck, pulling it out from under his shirt and letting the medal that hung from it drop against his chest. She remembered seeing the chain before, remembered wondering about its significance. Most operatives didn't wear impractical items, like jewelry, inside the complex. "I was under deep cover," he said. "That means no contact. None. It would have endangered the mission."

"The mission." Fury heated Anika's voice. "It's always going to come down to that, isn't it?" Hot tears scalded her eyes, burned the back of her throat. Maybe the agency was right to forbid romantic relationships. If Gianni were only her trainer, she wouldn't be angry about his absence, his distance. She might even be grateful to him for ensuring she followed through on a live kill, even if meant deceiving her to do it. "I don't think... I don't know how there can be more. With us." She turned to stalk off.

Gianni reached out.

She twisted away.

He caught hold of her arm and forced her to stop. "Contacting you would have...distracted me. Endangered not just the mission, but my life. I couldn't risk it. If I'd tried, I couldn't have done what was required."

Anika saw it then. The pain hiding behind his eyes. The sorrow he masked inside.

Her anger cooled, replaced by something warmer. Something that made her want to forget all about the agency's rule against emotional attachments.

She covered his hand with hers. If only she could soothe the pain away. "What did you have to do?"

He glanced away from her again, his gaze focused on a distant point. The same technique she had been taught to calm her emotions. His grip around her arm was a vise. "You were never far from my thoughts." His gaze returned to her face. "Believe that." Before Anika could speak, he released her and strode away.

She stood there, staring at him, as he became smaller and smaller. Her arm tingled with equal parts pain and pleasure. She rubbed the tender skin, certain he had left a mark.

Chapter 7

"Cheers!" Anika clinked her glass against Mari's and drained it. The potent cocktail, a Suicide Bomber, burned its way down her throat.

"Another?" Mari asked, and before Anika could answer, she had punched an order for a second round into their table's e-pad. She bobbed her head in time with the electro-world music blaring through Amnesia's sound system. The dozens of bronze braids from Mari's wig shimmied around her face. Her eyes shone with excitement and alcohol through her purple-tinted contacts. Full eye and lip makeup hid the facial bruises from her fight with the hostile. Her high-collared faux-fur top covered the flex-brace supporting her still-sore right shoulder. She looked happy and carefree. No doubt, the pain blockers from Clinic were working.

Anika had chosen to hide her own long dark hair under a wig of shoulder-length titanium blond waves. Her blue-green eyes were now a deep brown, her nose an upturned snub from temporary nasal implants, and her fair skin a sun-kissed bronze. She wore a short leather skirt, body-vest, and ankle boots. Shiny silver detachable sleeves wrapped around her arms past her elbows and hid the cast on her right wrist. To anyone watching, she looked like a young woman out for a night of fun. What she really wanted was a night of forgetting.

The disguises weren't absolutely necessary. Even if a bar regular spotted one of them using the street access to U.N.I.T's compound a few blocks away, they wouldn't understand they were witnessing a highly-trained operative reporting for duty at the world's most covert global counterterrorist agency. Still, better not to risk being recognized and possibly approached by a friendly civilian while so close to the agency.

Anika glanced around the bar's dim interior. Holograms of dancers intermixed with the human bodies shaking and weaving across the dance floor.

"Wanna groove?" Mari asked.

Anika shook her head. "Sure you're up for it? Not too sore from... today?"

"I'm sure."

Anika gestured toward the crowd. "Go for it."

A server-droid delivered their drinks. Mari took a big gulp of hers, then slid off her stool and salsa-stepped away.

Anika watched as her friend approached two guys standing on the edge of the floor, grabbed their arms, and pulled them into the gyrating mass. The bronze braids swung back and forth, as Mari swayed to the pulsing beat.

Anika smiled at the sight. Maybe Mari had the right idea. Apply a combination of alcohol, loud music, and dancing to unleash the tension and stress of the day. She took a sip of her drink and tried to enjoy the buzzing in her head and limbs. It had been so long since she had had a drink. Closing her eyes, she rocked side-to-side in her seat. How long?

An image of Gianni pressing a glass of champagne into her hand flashed through her mind. Her first mission. She had just rendezvoused with him at the North Korean embassy. They were overlooking the ballroom floor, pretending to be a couple at the exclusive social event. Though she had been too nervous to drink, he had insisted she hold a glass of the bubbly liquid to enhance her cover as a socialite enjoying herself. She had planned to drink some champagne after completing the assignment. But that plan changed with the shocking blare of the alarm followed by the heart-pounding escape through the building's temperature ducts.

Anika's eyes flew open, her hand clenched around the cocktail glass. She took a sip to ease her grip. That first mission had been terrifying. And thrilling. Especially those last precious minutes with Gianni, once she knew they had both escaped and the nano disc was safe. The glow of success had kindled inside her for weeks afterward.

Not like today. She swirled the purple-red liquid around in her glass. Today had been terrifying and sickening and confusing, with no afterglow. She'd thought she'd been acting to save Mari's life. But the grenade was fake and the syringe was full of saline. Mari hadn't been in mortal danger at all, and Anika had been deceived into shooting the hostile. All because Gianni believed she needed the proper motivation to kill.

Anika took a sip of her drink.

Maybe he was right. Maybe she couldn't just blindly follow kill orders. Did that make her a bad operative? Her hand tightened around the glass. She hoped not.

Mari weaved her way back to their table, her arm slung around a young woman's shoulders. Another dance partner?

"This is her," Mari cried out, flinging her arm toward Anika. "My savior."

Uh-oh, Anika thought. Her eyes widened in appraisal and apprehension. What had Mari done? Had she let her guard down and revealed something about U.N.I.T. she shouldn't have?

The woman nodded at Anika. She was Mari's height, 5'6", slender, with short hair streaked every color in the rainbow. Her eyebrows, arched above green eyes, matched her hair. "I'm Evan. How do you do?" Cut-glass British accent. Either a really good fake, or Evan belonged to

Britain's upper class.

"Hello," Anika replied, choosing to keep her name to herself. She set her glass on the table.

"Another round of Suicides?" Mari tapped the e-pad.

"God, no," Evan said. "Whiskey for me. Neat."

"I'm still working on mine," Anika said.

"Let me help." Giggling, Mari grabbed Anika's glass and drained it. She frowned at the glowing screen. "The pictures are swimming around on this thing. I think it's broken."

"Here, let me do it." Evan swiveled the e-pad away from Mari and gave it a few taps. "There. Done." She looked at Anika. "Nice work in the training facility today."

Anika's chest constricted. How would this woman know about what had happened in there today, unless Mari had told her?

"I'll say," Mari jumped in. "One shot. Right here," she continued, touching her forehead. "Bye-bye bad guy."

"Mari, stop." Anika's gaze traveled the room. Nobody seemed to be watching them and the music was certainly loud enough to swallow up their conversation. Still, agency business was not discussed in public or in front of strangers.

"It's okay," Mari said. "Evan's one of us."

"Anika's right," Evan said. "We need to be careful. Second probably has eyes and ears all over this place. Hacking into the droids' systems," she added, eyes narrowing at the e-pad. "Yes, that could work."

The combination of alarm and alcohol set off tiny explosions in Anika's brain. "How do you...who's Second?" She knew, of course. But she didn't know what this stranger in front of her knew.

Evan's left eyebrow lifted a half inch higher.

"I haven't seen you before," Anika said.

"Relax, Anika, baby." Mari squeezed Anika's hand. "Evan's cool-hot."

"Anika's right to question me," Evan said. "Trust no one, isn't that the training?" Anika didn't respond. "I transferred in from London a week ago. I'm the new number one in tech ops."

"I took Evan's advanced seminar in computer hacking while you were away on your last mission," Mari explained. "You should sign up. Girl's got some sweet tricks to teach."

Anika's chin lifted in challenge. "Describe Second."

"With pleasure." Evan leaned her arms on the table and looked straight at Anika. "Short, barely five feet. Bones like a bird, mind like a megacomputer. Blond hair. Similar to your color tonight, but not so... obvious," she said, a glint in her eyes.

"Ouch," Anika replied, in mock hurt.

"Don't get me wrong. I like your look. The ring's a nice bauble."

Anika fingered the thick leather band topped by an enormous skull on her left index finger.

"Looks a bit familiar," Evan said, continuing to eye the piece of jewelry. "A gift from the tech wizards at the agency?"

Hmm, yes. Anika crossed her arms and leaned forward, crushing the sparkly fabric of her sleeves against the table's surface.

The server arrived and set their drinks on the table. Anika waited until he was out of earshot before continuing. "You were describing Second."

"Blue eyes that cut right through you, like the stiletto heels she favors. Dresses smartly in bespoke suits. Comes across as being a posh, world-dominating executive. Which, in a way, I guess she is, given her number two position in the agency." Evan's lips quirked. "How'd I do?"

The description fit Second perfectly. "You didn't say anything a visual wouldn't show."

"Not even the description of her eyes? I thought that was rather poetic." Evan took a sip of her amber-colored drink. "Okay, I'll move on to Command," she said, mentioning the elusive top officer at the agency. "No current visuals of her floating around the ether. I met her

43

on my first day. Bald-headed, deep-voiced Amazon warrior. Probably didn't cut off one of her boobs so she could shoot an arrow better, unlike her ancient predecessors, though I wouldn't put it past her. Hard to be sure, though, given her preference for wearing loose tunics over long trousers." Evan set her glass down. "Convinced now?"

Evan's description of Command and their first-day meeting rang true. Anika had also seen Command on her first day at the agency. Along with the other recruits in her class, she had been taken to the tower office in Hub and introduced to the female commander who did, indeed, remind her of an Amazon.

"I thought Amazons cutting off their own breasts was a discredited myth," she said, still unsure about Evan.

"Hell of a myth, though, eh?" Evan grinned. When Anika didn't soften, she grew serious again. "Right, then. You joined U.N.I.T. six-oh-five thirteen months ago after being recruited from an orphanage in Washington, where you grew up. The orphanage belongs to the federal network that serves as one of the agency's two recruiting grounds. The other being, of course, life-row prison cells. So, you're known as a 'federal' in agency-speak. Unlike Mari." Evan took another sip. "And me."

"You're a lifer?" Mari sat up straight, her eyes beaming. "Like me?"

"Yes, like you, but for a different reason. Which I won't go into now," Evan said. "Need more?" She arched a rainbow-colored brow at Anika. "The first two alphas of your tracking ID are kilo, bravo."

Anika's gaze hardened. "You only know the first two?"

"Foxtrot, one, sev—"

"Enough." Anika cut her off. "How do you know so much about me?"

"Hacked your profile," Evan said. "I was curious about a recruit who completed her training and graduated to Level One in ten months, instead of the typical twelve," Evan replied. "Curious and impressed."

"No shit." Mari bobbed in her seat. "Anika kicks ass. And so do you." She saluted Evan with her glass before draining it and turning to Anika. "Evan's been running a sim for my next mission. Helping me prep so I don't fuck it up. You're both my heroes." Mari pointed at their mostly-full glasses on the table. "Finish up. Time for another round."

"You sure that's a good idea?" Anika asked. "Don't you have more rappelling practice or mission prep tomorrow?"

"Hey." Mari paused mid-bob. "Maybe we should all go rappelling tomorrow."

"Thank you, but no," Evan said. "I only exit down the sides of buildings in sims or holo-games. Using these." She wiggled her slender fingers.

"Hello, ladies." One of the two guys Mari had pulled onto the dance floor wedged in between her and Anika. Brown hair, medium height and build. Smelling of beer and sweat. "We've been looking for you." He gave a playful tug on one of Mari's braids. His friend stood a meter behind the table. "You left before the song ended."

"I got thirsty," Mari said.

"I'll buy you a drink, then. All of you." He grinned at Evan and Anika.

"Mega cool-hot." Mari beamed at him.

"Thanks, but we're leaving," Anika said.

Mari's smile morphed into a pout. "No, we're not."

"We have an early start tomorrow."

"You're not my trainer." Mari's pout hardened. "Or my superior. If I want another drink, I'll have one."

Her words stung Anika, a butterfly turned bee.

The guy slid his arm around Mari's waist. "That's what I like. A girl who knows her own mind."

"I didn't save your ass today so you could do something stupid tonight." Anika grabbed the edge of the table to hold herself in check.

"What happened today? How'd she save your ass?" The guy's arm slid lower. "Such a great ass, too."

"If we told you, we'd have to kill you," Mari said, then burst out laughing.

He spread his arms wide. "Take your best shot, baby."

Anika glowered at them.

He glanced at Anika, lips curling into a smirk. "Frost it, sweetheart. You're ruining the mood of our party."

Anika stood up from her seat. In her heeled boots, she cleared the creep's head. "I'm not your sweetheart. And the party's over."

"I have an idea." Evan walked around the table and inserted herself between Anika and the guy. "Let's take this party to my place. Just the three of us."

"I'm in," Mari said.

"What about him?" The guy jerked his head in the direction of his friend.

"Nah," Evan said. "My bed's not big enough for four."

The guy's eyes widened as Evan's words sunk in. He tossed back the rest of his drink and slammed the glass on the tabletop. "Let's go."

Mari slid off her seat, then flung her arm around the guy's neck to steady herself. "Whoops," she said, sagging against him.

He smashed his mouth down on hers.

Anika stepped around Evan, but the Brit blocked her with surprising speed and strength. Turning her head, she spoke in a low voice. "Don't worry. I've got this. He won't make it to my place."

"And Mari?"

"I'll make sure she arrives safe and sound in the morning."

"Get some Dry Out into her."

"Will do." Evan smiled. "You okay to get home on your own?"

"Yeah," Anika said. "Thanks."

Evan maneuvered herself between her companions, placed an arm around each of them, and steered them past the dance floor and to the other side of the bar.

"I guess it's just you and me now," the guy's friend said, leering.

Chapter 8

Tall and skinny with starched blond hair, he leaned against the table. His eyes looked glazed. He'd probably consumed something other than beer. "I'm JoJo."

"I'm leaving." Anika turned away from him.

JoJo grabbed her left hand. "Lemme buy you a drink."

Anika twisted out of his grasp, but he reached for her other hand. His fingers closed around the cast on her wrist. "Whoa, what you got under your sleeve there, babe?"

Her left hand fisted. A quick knuckle-jab to the throat would take him out. She'd have to change her position for a better approach. Even as she started to angle her body, her mind chanted *low profile, low profile*. There were other methods available to her. One of her instructors had often said, "With your looks, in the right situation, a soft smile can be more powerful than a hard punch."

"Are you guys okay?" A security-droid appeared at their table, his silver badge reflecting the room's lights. With his close-cropped hair, blue eyes, and strong jawline, he looked like a grown-up boy scout on super steroids.

JoJo bristled and tightened his hold on Anika. Fortunately, the cast's material hardened in response to the greater pressure and protected her wrist. "Get lost, robot," he snarled. "You're rotting the vibe."

Out of the corners of her eyes, Anika saw the heads of other patrons turned their way. *Shit.*

The droid fixed his gaze on her. "Ms?"

She curved her lips upward and stroked the guy's cheek. His baby-soft stubble tickled the backs of her fingers. "I'm fine." *I will be fine.* "But thank you for checking."

She kept her smile in place while the droid scanned her face and neck. "Your pulse is elevated."

"JoJo has that effect on me," she said, forcing a laugh and draping her arm around his neck.

Seconds passed. "Have a pleasant evening," the droid said, apparently satisfied that she was telling the truth. "And remember to..."

"...drink responsibly." JoJo talked over the droid's programmed parting message. "Yeah, yeah. Go back to your pen, now."

The droid pivoted a quarter turn and glided away.

"Dick 'bot," JoJo muttered, glaring after the droid.

Anika closed her eyes. She prepared herself for what she had to do next to get out of here with as little notice as possible. She took a breath, opened her eyes and placed her hand under JoJo's chin. Turned it so he faced her. Stroked his cheek. Leaned in. "How about we go someplace more private?"

JoJo grinned. "Hell, yeah." He tugged her closer and slid his hand up her thigh. "Your place or mine?"

Anika clamped down on his hand before it disappeared under her skirt, but held her smile steady. "Neither." His eyebrows creased in confusion. When he opened his mouth, she pressed her finger with the pirate-head ring against his lips. "I don't want to wait that long," she whispered into his ear. Then she bit down on his lobe, stopping short of drawing blood. He yelped and jerked back, cupping his ear. Her smile deepened. "Follow me." She pulled him toward a row of privacy pods farther back in the bar's interior.

They stopped outside the first one that showed a green light indicating vacancy. "I think fifteen minutes should do it, don't you? Unless you need more time?"

JoJo shook his head, then removed his handheld from his back pocket. It took him three tries to tap the buttons on his screen and wave it across the pod's payment scanner. Finally, the lock clicked and the door slid open. They ducked through the low opening into a dimly-lit space just big enough to fit a floor-level lounger with oversized pillows. The lounger's cover was torn at both corners and the deflated pillows looked as if their foam stuffing had worn out. A dozen liquor bottles cluttered the side wall shelf. A panic button glowed red on the wall. Music from the bar sounded through invisible speakers in a muffled pulse.

How romantic, Anika thought.

Standing in the narrow aisle between the couch and the shelf, she heard the scratch of a zipper behind her.

JoJo slid his arms around her waist and pressed his body against hers. Something hard nudged her ass.

It took all her self-control not to jam her elbow into his gut. Instead, she gave a low laugh, hooked her foot behind his, and leaned back. He fell onto the couch seat and she followed, landing on his lap. As his hands scrabbled at the buttons of her top, she twisted toward him and snuggled into his chest to force his hands to move to her back.

He jerked the hem of her top up and slid his hands down her bare skin. Her muscles rippled in protest in the wake of his touch. She dodged his mouth and sunk her lips into his neck.

He groaned in pain-pleasure.

Her hands twined around the back of his head. She turned the band of the ring so the skull faced down.

He pawed at the waistband of her skirt.

She heard the fastener rip and his breath quicken as he tried to tug her skirt off. She felt for the catch on the side of the skull. Released it to expose the microneedle inside. Jabbed it into his skin.

He gave a surprised grunt, then slumped back, his head falling to one side.

Anika jumped up and banged her hip against the edge of the shelf. Pain zinged up her side. She was breathing fast, her heart galloping. The walls of the tiny space seemed to close in on her.

She longed to flee, but worried about the security cams in the corridor outside capturing images of a panicked-looking woman. She smoothed her skirt back into place, re-buttoned her top, and mussed her hair. She should look a little ruffled. Her lungs filled and emptied with deep breaths until her pulse slowed. She closed the skull on the ring, turned the band so it faced outward again, and took another deep breath. *Thank you, tech geeks!*

Turning toward the shelf of liquor bottles, she eyed a few labels, and settled on one named Halcyon Daze. Her hands trembled as she removed the rectangular bottle of clear liquid. Opened it. Inhaled a sharp smell of alcohol and lime. Sprinkled some on JoJo's clothes and hair, then took a long swallow. It burned a trail down her throat. She took another.

She forced herself to wait several minutes before stomping out into the corridor and whirling to face the pod's open door. "Loser," she said, loud enough for the security cams to pick up. "Nothing worse than a guy who can't handle his shit." She shook her head as if disgusted, then strode off, concentrating on setting one foot in front of the other while she made her way back into the bar's main section, through the crowd, and out into the street.

Chapter 9

Twenty minutes later, Anika disengaged the locks on her apartment, stepped inside, and leaned back against the door. The loft was dark and quiet, with no street noise audible through the privacy screens covering the balcony doors. She had been living here since graduating to Level 1. It was her first non-institutional residence, her first apartment, her first real home. She loved every millimeter, from the tall ceilings to the wood-composite floors. It was chosen, paid for, and outfitted with essentials by the agency. These included high-end bath and kitchen appliances, a single lounge-seat with detachable table, and a media nook that projected scenic images onto a wall-sized monitor. A vista from the top of Mt. Everest at dawn appeared there now.

She had tried buying more furniture, but everything that looked familiar reminded her of the orphanage and everything that didn't felt like it didn't belong. Except for the oversized bed on the landing atop the winding staircase in the corner. That bed, with its luxe bedding and six pillows, was her one sure purchase and indulgence. She had bought it the same day she had been given the address and keycode. Right after she had completed her first mission and been informed of her promotion to Level 1 status.

She had entered the loft for the first time, thrown open the balcony doors, run up the circular stairs, then back down to the media center to start searching for the perfect bed. Brand-new, with a custom mattress and frame. Nothing like the saggy ones in the orphanage or the utilitarian ones in the recruits' quarters. As she considered different size and detail options, her mind kept replaying those last moments on the tarmac with Gianni. The feel of his hands on her waist, his lips on her mouth. She imagined the two of them in that bed, arms and legs wrapped around each other, and, with a shiver of anticipation, tapped the "buy now" button.

But that image of the two of them had remained only that. An image in her mind. Accompanied by a hundred other images that shadowed her throughout the days and nights of his absence. Everywhere she went, both inside and outside the agency, she saw Gianni. Turning a corner in a corridor, crossing a threshold into a conference room, weaving through a street crowd, standing in line for a morning espresso. Even tonight, as she was leaving the bar, she'd thought she had seen him near the exit. All phantom sightings.

Regret mixed with longing, a bitter cocktail inside her.

She tilted her head to rest it against the door. Closed her eyes. *Mistake.* Dizziness forced her eyes open. She peeled off the detachable sleeves, letting the air cool her bare arms. As she brought her fingers to her temples, a sound between a sigh and a groan escaped her lips. Those additional sips—no, gulps—of liquor had caught up with her.

Now she really regretted not having a couch in the living area. She could stretch out on the day-lounger but it wasn't as comfortable as the bed. But to get there, she would have to climb the winding set of stairs that now seemed impossibly steep.

She shoved away from the wall.

The door chime rang from the security panel. A zing of alarm shot through her. She stopped mid-stride. Who could that be at this hour? Had something happened to JoJo at the bar? She hadn't checked his pulse before leaving him. Had the mix of beer, whatever other substance he had taken, and the drug in her ring been too much for his body to take? Had the police tracked her down to question her?

She jabbed at the panel button to activate visual. Her eyes widened and her pulse quickened. Not the police. She spoke into the mic. "What are you doing here?" Her voice shook, a leaf quivering in a strong wind.

"May I come in?" Gianni's brown eyes bored into hers through the monitor.

She had wanted this moment to happen for so long. Had dreamed of him standing at her door, asking to come in. Now that he was here, a cold touch of anxiety embraced her. Surely, he hadn't shown up in the middle of the night, unannounced, to pick up where they had left off three months ago.

Had the agency been surveilling her at Amnesia? Was she in trouble for using the skull ring outside of an authorized mission?

She pressed the release button and the exterior door to her building opened. Gianni stepped through it.

"Is something wrong?" she asked as soon as Gianni crossed the threshold into her apartment.

His gaze traveled up the wall, across the ceiling, to the staircase in the corner, then back to her. "Nice place."

She stood close to the wall in case her head started to spin again.

"Are you all right?" He glanced at her cast. "How's your wrist?"

Her brows drew together. "I...it's...I'm fine."

"You looked shaken as you left the bar. Your stride was unsteady."

"You...saw me at Amnesia? You were there?"

Gianni nodded. "You appeared to be enjoying yourself with Mari and Evan. And the men who joined you." His gaze was hard, his stance rigid.

Was he *angry*? Her muscles tightened. After all these months of making her wait and wonder where he was, whether he was coming back, now *he* was angry?

Her eyes narrowed. "You followed us?"

"Just you."

"Since when?"

"You're a Level One. You tell me." His eyes flared in anger, twin fires igniting.

Anika's mind flashed to the image she had seen as she neared the bar's exit. Dark blond hair, broad shoulders, leather jacket. A man of Gianni's height and build angled away from her, standing at a waist-high counter. Tube of water at his elbow. She had noticed it, then told herself to forget it. Like all the other phantom images of the past months. Only this time, apparently, the image had been real.

"You were standing at a counter near the exit. At my ten o'clock."

"I wanted to make sure you were all right after what happened today."

"You mean after you forced me to kill a human being?"

"If that's how you want to see it, then, yes." His voice chilled even as his eyes continued to burn.

"How else am I supposed to see it?"

"As a chance to prove that you can do what needs to be done. You want to stay with the agency, yes?"

The question hit her, a fist to the gut. She braced her hand against the wall. It felt cool and firm beneath her palm. God, yes, she wanted to stay. She nodded in mute agreement.

"I sent the security-droid. At the bar."

Anika's mouth dropped open. "Why?"

"It looked like you needed help."

Irritation scratched the back of her neck. "I was trying to keep a low profile. Sending the droid only made it worse. If you thought I needed help—which I didn't, by the way—why didn't *you* come?"

"Because if I had, I would *not* have kept a low profile."

Anika's brows lifted. She stared into Gianni's eyes. The heat there wasn't only anger. He was *jealous*. The realization sent a shivery thrill up her spine. She loved knowing she could stir such a strong emotion in him. "Well," she said, blowing out a breath, "I handled the droid. And the guy."

"How exactly did you 'handle the guy'?"

Resentment flared, like a fast-spreading rash. Why did he deserve to know? "Are you asking for professional reasons or personal ones?"

"Can't you guess?"

"I'd like to hear you say it."

He huffed out a breath. "Personal." He turned his hands toward her, palms out, in supplication. "Please. Parlami." The words in Italian—*talk to me*—caressed her, landing like a kiss on her cheek.

She softened, her irritation receding.

"I tried to blow him off and leave. When that didn't work, I took him into a private pod, let him paw at me while I maneuvered into position, and then jabbed him with this." She sprung open the skull on the ring to reveal the microneedle inside. "Borrowed it from the tech lab at the agency."

"How much pawing took place?" Gianni's tone was grim.

"Not much," Anika said, shaking her head. "No clothes were removed during the...um, encounter."

"The guy sounds like an amateur."

"Lucky for me."

"Lucky for *him*," Gianni replied, his voice tight.

Their eyes met.

The heat in his gaze was fueled by something different than anger, but equally primal. Possessiveness. Desire.

Anika's skin prickled in response. She wanted to feel his skin on hers; she didn't care if she got burned. She pushed away from the wall and stumbled toward him.

He caught her by the shoulders, steadied her.

She leaned against him and wrapped her arms around his neck. He felt as solid as the wall. Only much, much nicer to hold onto, even if his nearness made her head spin more than the alcohol. "I should have said *yes*." She pressed her lips to his.

His mouth parted and his arms closed around her, setting off sparks.

She drew back. Took his face, his gorgeous face, between her hands. "*Yes*," she repeated, drinking in the sight of him, delighting in the feel of him. "On the tarmac. *Yes.* To the café. *Yes.* To us. I'm saying *yes* now." She buried her face in his chest, reveling in the warmth of his hands at her waist. "Yes, yes, yes." She couldn't seem to stop saying it. She'd waited so long to be able to say it, and wanted to be sure he heard her now. She needed him to know how much she wanted him.

He placed his hand under her chin and tilted her head up. "I'll help you upstairs."

"Yes, yes, yes." Fireworks of joy and desire exploded inside her. Her dream was coming true. Gianni was here, with her, in her apartment. He was holding her hand, leading her up the stairs, toward the bed she had bought for the two of them. She started laughing. "Yes, yes, yes." He led her higher and higher. Then he was helping her sit down on the edge of the bed, taking off her boots, swinging her legs up and over. She stretched her arms overhead, sighed, and closed her eyes. They were entering the best part of the dream. The part where he would take off the rest of her clothes, then his own, then lie down next to her. Or, better yet, on top of her. Press her body into the mattress with the weight of his own. She would wrap her legs around him, mold her body to his. "Yes, yes, yes."

"Drink this."

Her eyes blinked open. It took a moment for her vision to clear. She saw the bottle of Dry Out in Gianni's outstretched hand. He still had his clothes on. So did she. "Wha—"

He brought the glass to her lips and tipped its contents into her mouth.

The taste of cherry chalk coated her tongue and cheeks. She shuddered and swallowed.

He set the bottle on the attached side table. "Remember, briefing at oh-six-hundred hours." Then he returned to the head of the stairs and disappeared down into the darkness.

Chapter 10

"Cut! Cut!" The director of the sex vid sounded exasperated. "Take five. We'll go again."

The room's lights brightened. The director jumped up from his chair and led his crew of three—visual engineer, sound technician, and wardrobe consultant—out of the room.

Anika lay back on the bed and snugged the sheets around her almost-naked body.

Before the shoot had started, the wardrobe consultant had applied ThickSkin spray-on material to her ass and her pelvis, below her hip bones. When Anika had asked for more covering, the woman's hot-pink eyebrows scrunched together as she seemed to be considering the request. After a quick nod, she got to work decorating Anika's breasts with a multi-colored serpent design, then spritzed her with a bronze mist, touched up her lip stain, and announced, "She's ready."

Now, Anika didn't know if she wanted to cry or to scream. Or to strangle the operative, Guang Lin, who lay next to her. They had been rehearsing for more than two hours and, so far, had nothing to show for it.

"I'm sorry," Lin whispered.

She looked over at the man who was her partner on her newest mission. His pale skin looked even paler in the bright lighting. Sweat beaded his scalp, visible through his dark spiky hair. A wet trickle ran down the side of his face. He was a Level 1 operative from her same class. She had sparred with him a few times during fight training. He had some decent moves, but once she had learned how to counter them, he never won a match against her. She didn't remember him excelling in any of her other classes or seminars, and, at the time, she had doubted he would graduate. Apparently, she had been wrong.

They had been briefed this morning, then ordered to report here to start preparations for their upcoming mission as undercover husband-and-wife assassins who had been married for two years. They had been informed they would need a souvenir video, a sexual one, to add credibility to their cover. Most couples, married or not, stored at least one sex vid on their handhelds and/or in their personal archives. Some recorded their first time together as casually as they recorded their first date, first kiss, first house, and first child. Others held off on a sex vid until they were serious about each other, even waiting until their honeymoon to make one as a symbol of their commitment to each other.

Anika had recorded a few kissing videos with the other kids, both guys and girls, in the orphanage. They had been innocent adolescent experiments. But there were no recordings of her experiences with lovemaking. She didn't want a tangible reminder of the disappointing ones, including her first with a popular boy in her class who admitted, after a rushed and unsatisfying encounter, she was his first "federal." Those worth remembering, she preferred to relive in her mind rather than on screen.

When she had learned at the briefing that shooting a mock sex vid was part of mission prep, Anika's stomach had clenched in dismay. She didn't want to do it. While her trainers had discussed the potential need for these kinds of videos as part of fieldwork, no recruit had been required to make them during training. The agency was more focused on fighting and shooting and surveillance drills.

Lin had seemed equally dismayed at the mention of a mock sex vid. He had tried to object by questioning how a video could be made *today*, with an accurate timestamp, when, in reality, their aliases' souvenir sex vid would likely have been recorded earlier in their two-year relationship.

The briefing agent had been dismissive, even belittling, in his response. "Because we'll *scrub* the date and time indicators. I'm surprised you don't remember that from your training. Any more dumb questions?"

Anika had charged out of the room, with Lin trailing behind. If they had to record a mock a sex vid, she wanted to get it over with.

She knew she didn't have a choice. The briefing agent was right. Having a sex vid *would* strengthen their backstory as a married couple. They might even need a variety of souvenir videos to "document" their relationship history. The thought of recording multiple fake romantic scenarios with Lin made Anika cringe, but she couldn't afford to object. She had narrowly escaped discipline, or worse, for her failure to shoot during the Belgrade mission. She had to prove herself with this new mission. That meant no protests, no refusals, no missteps.

The director and his three-person team had all tried coaching Anika and Lin through their miming various moves in an attempt to capture realistic-looking foreplay and intercourse.

Lin was a terrible performer. Awkward in the extreme, his arms and legs twitched and jerked like a malfunctioning toy robot with every cue by the director. He had gotten hard and ejaculated within two minutes of climbing into bed with Anika.

She had tried to be sympathetic. Lin didn't want to be here anymore than she did. And her own performance wasn't much better than his. She couldn't seem to stop her muscles from tensing every time his skin touched hers. But, in the moment, all she had felt was queasy and resentful at the delay. She wanted to put this embarrassing, uncomfortable session behind her as quickly as possible.

After Lin had cleaned up, they had tried again. And again.

Finally, in frustration, the director had ordered endorphin shots for both of them. But the induced euphoria didn't translate to persuasive passion on screen.

At one point, the director had yelled, "No, no! You're about as convincing as first gen droids."

Now, as she lay next to Lin, Anika wondered what she could do to at least improve her own acting. Earlier, she had tried pretending Lin was the man she really wanted beside her. Bad idea.

When she had closed her eyes and conjured an image of Gianni's face, she remembered what had happened the previous night. How she had clung to him, saying *yes, yes, yes* over and over, like a schoolgirl with her first crush, only to be humiliated when he escorted her upstairs to her giant bed and then left her alone in it. She had lain awake, staring at the ceiling, until 0300 hours when she had finally taken a soother. The two hours of sleep before the alarm jolted her awake had helped, but fatigue still pulled on her, like weights made of osmium attached to her limbs.

She wanted nothing more than to roll onto her side, curl into a ball, and drop into a dreamless sleep. But if she did that, it would be over. She would fail the mission, the agency, herself. Not going to happen. Not after she had worked so hard to be chosen, to belong. She had to help Lin get over his discomfort. Get him out of his head and into his body. Then, let nature take over. Resolve chased away her fatigue.

"Lin," she whispered. "It's okay. There's nothing to be sorry about. This prep is really hard. But if we work together, I know we can do it." Lin didn't respond. "Come on. Look at me." He turned his head, but his gaze landed somewhere above her shoulder. "No, Guang, look at *me*." His frightened-animal gaze skittered down her face, shot back up, then down again, then back up. She lay still until his gaze finally settled. "It won't be long before they come back. Forty-four seconds, I think."

"Forty-one," he said, machine-like.

Clearly, Lin had been practicing his time tracking. She was still working on perfecting her technique. "Right. Forty-one. It's just us now. No one else. No camera, no crew, no director. So, relax and sync your breathing with mine. In-two-three. Out-two-three."

"Why?" Lin asked.

Anika's lips compressed. "Just do it. In-two-three. Out-two-three." She watched Lin's chest expand and contract in time with her breath count. "That's it. Keep going. Whatever happens, just keep breathing." She rolled onto her side and scooted closer to him. His eyes widened and his nostrils flared, but his breathing stayed even. "Good. In-two-three." She rested her hand on his chest. "Out-two-three. I'm going to place my lips on yours. In-two-three. Out-two-three. And when I do, open your mouth a little and...taste me. Okay?"

Lin's gaze locked on her mouth as if it was a lethal weapon.

"Look at me. Watch me." His gaze moved up. He had nice eyes, she noticed. Light brown, with a gold rim around the pupil. "Keep breathing." She lowered her head until their lips touched.

Pain, hot and sharp, shot through her lower lip. Anika reared back. "Ouch," she yelped. "I said 'taste,' not 'bite.'" She pressed her fingers to her mouth and wiped away blood. Her lower lip was already starting to swell.

The door opened, and the video crew filed back inside. "What the hell?" the director yelled.

Anika looked up and froze.

Gianni had joined them. "Are you all right?" he asked. His tone was professional, but Anika detected a flash of concern in his gaze. At least, she hoped she did.

She pulled the bed sheet around her and nodded.

"What happened?" the director asked, arms crossed, legs wide.

"We were trying to...relax-sh." The last word came out with an extra syllable from Anika's swollen lip.

"This isn't supposed to be a rough sex vid," the director said. "Although, at this point, I'd settle for anything that looked halfway decent."

"Let me see." Gianni walked over to the monitor. "Play back," he ordered. The light from the monitor shone on Gianni's face as he watched a few minutes of the session. His expression remained impassive.

Anika sank onto her haunches. Sweat rivulets slid down her back. She wanted to disappear from embarrassment. What was Gianni thinking as he watched her with Lin? Did she look like a complete amateur? Last night, he had been jealous when he saw her with JoJo at the bar. Was he jealous now? Or did he consider this just part of the job? She couldn't detect any emotion from him.

Gianni looked up from the monitor. "Lin, report to the sim lab."

Lin didn't move.

"Now," Gianni said.

Anika nudged him.

Lin bolted from the bed, into his clothes, and out the door.

"We were making progress," Anika said.

Gianni studied her puffy lip. "Yes, I can see that."

Annoyance darted through her. Did he think this was easy for her? Had he ever made a mock sex vid?

"Give us time," she said. "We'll get there."

"There's no more time. We're going with a different scenario."

"What scenario?"

"I'm replacing Lin."

Anika's pulse jet rocketed. She tightened the sheets around her. *God, no. Please, no.* "You are?"

Gianni turned to the wardrobe consultant. "Get me ready."

"Behind there," the woman replied, nodding at the hinged dark screen in the corner of the room. "Everything off."

Gianni disappeared behind the screen. The consultant followed.

The engineer and the director huddled near the camera and monitor, murmuring back and forth.

Anika wished the bed would swallow her so she could escape what was coming. *Not like this*, she thought. *Not for our first time.* For months, she had dreamed of being with Gianni, in bed, their arms and legs wrapped around each other. This was as far from that dream as she could imagine. Their first time, taking place in front of a film crew, being recorded as cover for a mission in which they were pretending to be other people. Assassins. Contract killers. Her stomach churned and she prayed she wouldn't be sick.

The wardrobe consultant reappeared and approached Anika, a tube in her hand. "I need to fix that lip." The woman dabbed a gel that smelled of honey and disinfectant on Anika's lip. The pain and throbbing vanished. She applied more lip stain, studied Anika through narrowed eyes, and nodded. "That'll do," she said.

Gianni stepped out from behind the screen.

Anika's gaze darted across his face, chest, groin, and legs. He wore nothing except for some ThickSkin over his groin. Even the silver chain was gone from his neck. Her quick scan had confirmed a glorious image of taut muscles, sharp angles, and smooth hollows. She couldn't bring herself to look into his eyes. Instead, her gaze fixed on his bare feet. They looked solid, strong, with well-defined tendons extending from the base of each toe.

"Where do you want me?" Gianni asked the director.

"Behind her. Start by kissing her neck and shoulder. We'll go from there."

Anika watched Gianni's feet pad across the floor toward the bed until they disappeared from her peripheral vision. Her fingers clenched the sheets so tightly they started to cramp. The mattress dipped as Gianni sat on it. She could feel the heat from his body warm her back.

"Action," the director said.

Gianni's lips brushed the right side of her neck.

Anika jerked and gasped.

"Cut," the director said.

Gianni pulled away.

"Sounds are okay," the director said, "as long as they convey you're enjoying yourself. Not that you're being tortured. Got it? Let's go again. Action."

Gianni spoke into her ear. "Close your eyes. Pretend it's just us."

Anika turned her head to look into his eyes, searching for the man inside the operative. For a few precious heartbeats, she found him. It reassured her. Maybe she would be able to go through with this after all. She let her lids fall shut.

This time, when his lips touched her skin, Anika focused on the dual sensations of pressure and warmth. His nearness caused her pulse to quicken, her heart to pound. Her head rolled back against his shoulder and she gave a soft moan. As his lips planted open-mouthed kisses along her neck and shoulder, her mind cried out *yes, yes, yes*. She flashed back to last night when she had said that word. Out loud. Over and over. Waves of remorse and humiliation rose inside her and doused the glow from Gianni's touch. Her head snapped upright.

"Cut!" the director yelled.

Anika squeezed her eyes shut and knocked her fist against her forehead. "Sorry," she muttered.

The mattress dipped and rose as Gianni stood and walked over to the director.

Anika scrambled out of the bed, dragging the sheet with her. She stood against the wall, and tried to recall the calming techniques from her bio psych seminars. She concentrated on a mark in the paint and forced her breath to slow to an even count. In, out, in, out, in, out.

After a few minutes, the crew started packing up the equipment and Gianni stepped back behind the screen.

"What's going on?" Anika asked. "Aren't we going to try again?"

Gianni reappeared. He had changed back into his dark pants and T-shirt. A length of silver chain peeked out from the neckline. He approached her. "How's your wrist?"

"What? My...it's fine. Don't we need to try again? I can do this." Anika grabbed his arm, letting the sheet slip from her shoulders. "Please."

"How much function have you recovered in your wrist?"

"Eighty-eight percent."

His gaze tracked over her, seeming to catalog every drop of dried sweat, every line of fatigue. She must have looked like hell.

"Do another PT session," he said. "Study up on your alias. Get some sleep, a solid eight hours at least. Or spend time in a relaxation tank."

"What about the vid?" she asked.

"We'll try again tomorrow."

Anika wanted to object, wanted to say they should try again *now*. But the will to fight left her, air expelled from a blown-out tire. She didn't have the energy to argue. Or the strength to risk more failure. Maybe Gianni was right. Maybe they'd have better success tomorrow.

Chapter 11

Anika spent the rest of the day in nonstop activity to keep her mind from hopscotching from one disturbing image to another. The hostile's lifeless body. Mari's swollen eye. Lin's stricken face. Gianni's impassive gaze.

After an extra-long session of physical therapy, including the electro-osteo stimulator, the machine confirmed her wrist had returned to ninety-two percent function. Post-session, she had taken a double dose of pain blockers to calm her throbbing wrist. En route to the relaxation tank, she changed directions. The thought of all that darkness and stillness, with nothing but painful memories from the past two days for company, filled her with dread.

She left the complex and returned to her loft apartment. She programmed the details of her alias—name, date and place of birth, parents' names, home address, educational background, etc.—into her sound system and set it on an audio loop so she could memorize the backstory. She listened and absorbed the information while completing a ninety-minute workout followed by a hot shower. Clean and alert, she returned to the living area, paused audio, and settled into a cross-legged position in front of the wall screen. From there, she called up an image of a flickering candle. "Focus your gaze and the mind will follow," her meditation instructor had said. But her mind didn't follow. Not today.

It kept buzzing from flashback to flashback, like a pollinating bee.

She gave up. Glanced at the staircase that led to her bedroom and thought about trying to get some sleep. The memory of staring at her ceiling, wide-eyed and sleepless, from the previous night had her walking over to the day-lounger instead. She slid into its contoured seat, activated her media system, and rotated through dozens of entertainment channels, occasionally pausing on chase scenes in action movies, highlights of sports matches, updates of global news, and the finales of home decorating shows. A couple of hours in, her grumbling stomach reminded her she hadn't eaten anything that day other than a protein bar. After checking her carb and fat credit balance, she placed an order of a childhood favorite, mac 'n' cheese, with a local eatery. She ate every bite, then resumed channel-shuffling until the sun settled low in the sky.

Following a tip from the winner of the home decorating show, she scrolled through a furniture website in search of the perfect couch. Forty-five minutes later, she finalized the purchase of a sleek, modern two-seater in a color described as Asiana Plum. With a satisfying sigh, she lay back in the day-lounger, resumed the audio loop about her alias, and closed her eyes. Soon, the combination of a full stomach, the warmth from the heated seat, and the drone of the computerized voice lulled her to sleep.

The buzz of the doorbell jolted her back to consciousness. Lights shone from the windows in the residential tower across the street. Between the two buildings, the sky was black, like a shade had been drawn across them. The numbers on the media system glowed 2100. She had been asleep a little over two hours. Not nearly long enough. She groaned and pushed herself to standing.

"Computer, shut down audio." The loop cut off. "Activate monitor for outdoor camera." Anika approached the screen to see who was bothering her this time of night.

The figure standing there caused the breath to hitch in her throat. *Again?* For a second night in a row, Gianni stood on her doorstep. The sight of him chased away her grogginess. Her heartbeat shifted from steady to staccato.

What now? Hadn't she been through enough today? She glanced down at her thick black tights, tank top, and cream wraparound sweater, and wondered if she had time to change back into her standard-issue unisuit and fitted jacket.

The bell buzzed a second time. *Screw it.* He hadn't given her advance notice. This was her place. She could dress as she liked. She blew out a breath, smoothed her hands through her hair, and disengaged the lock.

When Gianni entered the apartment, she crossed her arms against her chest. "Let me try again," she said. "With Lin. Give me two hours with him. Alone. We'll make a self-vid."

"It will look amateurish. Wealthy people, including well-paid assassins, don't create their own vids."

"Then give me a couple of hours to rehearse with him. I...we...can do it."

Gianni set the soft-sided metallic bag slung over his shoulder down on the floor. He slid out of his jacket and tossed the garment on the lounger. "I'm standing in for Lin. It's been decided."

Alarm twisted knots in Anika's stomach. She knew she had been wrong to think she would have better success tomorrow with the sex vid. She wouldn't be able to control her body's response to Gianni. Even now, separated by a full meter's distance, his presence acted like shock waves, setting off reverberations inside her. The thought of going back into that room, with the staged bed, the almost-naked costume, and the critical eye of the director, made her want to flee. She wouldn't be able to go through with it.

"Why was Lin chosen for the mission anyway?" Anxiety sharpened the tone of her voice. "How did he even graduate to Level One?"

"He speaks twelve languages."

"I thought we used translation implants for that."

"They're not always practical in the field. He's also proven himself an effective sniper." Gianni's eyes met—and held—hers. "Accurate, cool-headed, fires without hesitation."

That brought Anika up short. Tendrils of doubt swirled through her. "Why was I chosen?" The question came out in a whisper.

"You're an excellent shot. And Second believes you'll be persuasive as the female half of a husband-and-wife team of assassins. If paired with the right operative."

Anika's pulse skipped a beat. "And Second thinks you're the right one...I mean, operative, for me?"

"She does." A smile spread across Gianni's lips, a heart-melting contrast from the somber expressions he had worn since his return. He walked toward her.

With every step, every shortening of the distance between them, Anika's pulse quickened. If she didn't know for certain that her body hadn't moved, she'd swear she'd just completed a sprint.

She shook her head. "I don't think I can...do it. Fake a performance in front of a camera. Not..." Her voice trailed off. *Not with you.*

Gianni took her hand and brought it to his mouth. He pressed his lips against her fingers, which felt cold in his warmth. "I don't want to fake a performance, either. Especially not for our first time."

Despite Anika's best efforts, tears filmed her eyes. "What are we going to do?"

"Computer," Gianni called out, "play a ballad." A whiskey-timbered female voice crooned through the speakers. Gianni slid his arms around Anika. "May I have this dance?"

Chapter 12

Anika held back, keeping space between their bodies, afraid he would feel her heart thudding against her ribs. "This is the second night in a row you've come here. Won't that raise questions?"

"My tracker is offline. The agency doesn't know I'm here."

"You can do that?"

"As a Level Three, yes. For six hours. Any more questions?"

Anika shook her head. She was out of ideas for how to keep Gianni at a distance. At this point, she didn't know if she wanted to anyway.

"Relax," he murmured against her ear, his breath a warm summer breeze.

Part of her wanted to do as he said. It felt delicious to be this close to him. It was a moment she had dreamed about during his long absence. But after last night, when she had made it humiliatingly clear how much she wanted him, and he had simply left, she wasn't sure she trusted him. Or herself around him. If she let her guard down, and he wounded her again, she didn't know what she would do. Still, she couldn't bring herself to say anything. The hurt from last night was too fresh, too raw.

As if reading her mind, or maybe noting the stiffness of her arms, Gianni said, "Last night, when I left, it was one of the hardest things

I've ever done."

Surprised by his admission, she stared into his eyes. "It was?"

He nodded. Firmed his grip around her.

"Why didn't you stay?"

"After what happened in the training facility, your anger with me, I needed some time. I wasn't ready."

Anika stopped moving and took hold of his arms. "And now?"

"And now," Gianni said, drawing a deep breath, "I don't want to wait any longer." He pulled her closer. "Do you?"

In answer, her body softened into his embrace.

The music floated over them, enveloped them, as Gianni led her around the room. He twirled her in a slow circle. She stumbled, but he caught her in time, laughing. The sound, a husky rumble, sent sparks down to her toes. "Like the night at the embassy. Remember?"

"How can I forget?" Anika said. Her first mission. Their first mission together. "At least that night I had an excuse. Those platform-heeled shoes were impossible."

"We should practice dancing more often."

As the final notes of the song drifted through the air, Anika expected Gianni would request another. Instead, he released her and walked over to the bag on the floor, where he removed a bottle of champagne and two long-stemmed flutes. "Twenty forty-five. An excellent year." He uncorked the champagne and poured the pale gold liquid into the glasses. "Let's toast to the impending success of our mission." He tapped her glass with his—*clink*—and drank.

The bubbles tickled her nose and throat.

Gianni refilled her glass. "Computer, play another ballad." With the bottle in one hand, he trailed his other down her back. "Drink up," he said.

Three songs later—or was it four—the first bottle was empty and the second one uncorked.

They continued to dance, but their movements slowed. Their feet grazed the floor. Their bodies swayed in a languorous rhythm. Cool sips of champagne interspersed with heated kisses. The combination made Anika's head swim.

"I think I need to sit," she said.

"I have a better idea." Gianni pressed his lips to the curve of skin where her neck and shoulder met. He slid his mouth up to her ear, where he tickled her lobe with his tongue, drawing forth gasps of pleasure. "Let's go upstairs." Holding onto the half-consumed bottle of champagne, he took Anika's hand in his and led her toward the circular staircase. As they ascended, Gianni called out, "Computer, continue playing ballads."

At the landing, Gianni's kisses grew deeper, longer, wetter.

Shivers of desire coursed through Anika.

"Cold?" Gianni murmured, before pressing yet another open-mouthed kiss on the side of her neck.

Anika shook her head. "Not at all." She closed her eyes to better focus on the sensations his mouth and hands sparked inside her.

"Good." Gianni set down the champagne and glasses on the end table. "Okay if I loosen this?" He touched the knotted belt on her sweater. She nodded. He slid the garment off her shoulders and down her arms. It fell to the floor at their feet. "And this?" He reached for the hem of her tank top, pulled it over her head. As his hands slid down her bare back and drew her close against him, his mouth found hers for another lingering kiss.

"Computer, turn off lights," Anika said.

The loft darkened.

"I want to see you." Gianni eased her onto the bed. "Computer, set ambient lights at thirty percent." A warm glow suffused the room. His gaze wandered at leisure over her face, down her throat, across her breasts, and down her torso.

He straddled her. With the bottle champagne in hand, he dribbled a

74

few drops on her stomach.

She gasped as the cold liquid touched her heated skin.

He bent lower and licked off the champagne. His lips moved up her torso to her breasts, where he took one, then the other into his mouth. Anika's back arched up, inviting him to take more, do more. He took a sip of champagne and brought his mouth to hers, opening it, releasing the liquid into hers. It fizzed on her tongue, along the inside of her cheeks, an explosion of tiny bubbles. His tongue found hers. Probed, tasted.

Her legs wrapped around him, pulling him closer. Her arms grabbed his shirt, tugged it up. He leaned back a little so she could remove the barrier of fabric separating bare skin from bare skin. When she did, the silver chain that he always wore swung in the air between them. He flattened it against his chest before lying on top of her, his mouth finding hers once more.

His weight, his heat, felt so right. They helped satisfy the craving that had built inside of her during his absence. But they weren't enough. "More," she whispered.

Gianni lifted his head to meet her gaze. His lips quirked. "More what? Champagne?"

"More...everything." She reached for the waistband of his pants, tugged at his zipper, slipped her fingers inside. More heat there, along with a thrilling hardness. Her touch resulted in a quick inhale from Gianni.

She reveled in the sound, delighted at his response.

He snagged her waistband and, with a fluid movement, stripped off her tights. His pants followed. Back on top of her, he made her feel every millimeter of his body. Mouth on hers, hands under her ass, lifting her, positioning her. He slid into her. Hot, sweet pressure.

"More," she panted. At first, he gave several slow thrusts, like the tempo of the ballads, but then the pace increased. Medium tempo.

"More." Fast tempo. Again and again, faster and faster, until she was breathless, until she was faint. "More." He twined his fingers in hers, giving more until they both cried out in release.

Gianni rolled off her, pulling her with him. They lay facing each other while their breaths slowed back down to ballad tempo. He traced his finger along the side of her face, down her jaw, across her lips. "That's what I wanted for our first time."

She brushed her lips against his fingers. This moment was like her birthday—the one day of the year in the orphanage when she got a sugar high from cake and ice cream and fizzy drinks and felt as if she could fly. "Know what I want?" she asked.

His brows rose, dark wings perched above bemused eyes.

Her hand rested on his chest. His heart pulsed against her palm. Strong, steady, alive. "Lie back." She reached for the champagne from the night stand and checked its weight. Still a quarter full. Smiling, she splashed some on Gianni. "More."

* * *

Anika awoke in an empty bed. Early morning sun washed across the skylight. The sheets were still warm where Gianni had lain next to her. She pressed her face into the soft fabric and breathed in his scent. She hadn't heard him leave. Disappointment sapped her energy. The night had passed too soon. The sugar high was long gone, and she had crashed back to earth.

She spied a bottle of Dry Out on the side table. Her lips twisted. Had Gianni left it out of genuine concern, or because he wanted her sharp for the day ahead? Her handheld sat next to the bottle. Strange. She didn't remember bringing it up from downstairs. The side button blinked to indicate an unread e-note. She reached for the device.

"Change in plans," the note from Gianni said. "Report to Wardrobe, then to Transport. I'll meet you there. Wheels up at 0900 hours." Anika re-read the note. No mention of a sex vid. How could that be? The next sentence eased the pang of his absence. "Last night was beyond all imaginings."

Six simple words that told her last night hadn't been a dream. Even better, it had meant as much to him as it had to her.

Following that sentence was a final one. "As soon as you've read this, hit delete."

Flashes of memory, images caught in a strobe light, erupted in her mind. She lay back and let them play across the undersides of her eyelids. Her body grew warm and wet from the mini-replays of the previous night.

Gianni was right. Their first time had been better than her imagination had conjured. Still, she wanted more than simply memories.

She deleted the message. All but those six words. Those, she saved in an encrypted file.

Chapter 13

"Let's review it again," Gianni said. "Start with our names."

Anika inhaled a deep breath and exhaled to a count of three. She had twice recounted the details of their aliases, even remembering to switch up the choice of words to make it sound unrehearsed. Was a third time really necessary?

"We're Antonio and Lena Bianchi," she said. "We've known each other a little over two years. We met during a job when, unbeknown to either of us, a client hired us both to carry out the same hit. We married six weeks later." Anika ran her thumb around the platinum band on her left ring finger. Thinner than the one Gianni wore, it felt strange against her skin. Like it didn't belong there, even though the size was a perfect fit. The wardrobe consultant had handed it to her along with the silver studs for her ears. They were the finishing touches of her outfit, a metallic gray unisuit, the legs tucked into mid-calf leather boots.

"Go on," Gianni prodded.

"No kids," she said. "Too risky, given our line of work."

She and Gianni were sitting side-by-side in the contoured seats of one of the new hover planes owned by the agency. The aircraft had the distance and speed capability of a classic jet plane, with the vertical landing capability of a helicopter. In the cockpit, Agent Diego Santos piloted the aircraft. They were flying to El Salvador.

Anika tapped her foot against the floor to dispel the nervous energy coursing through her. She was revved. Had been ever since she had boarded. But she wasn't certain of the cause. Was it the mission, or the man beside her? Gianni's knee bumped hers as the plane dipped and rose in the sky. A spark shot through her leg and up her side. She shifted in her seat to create more space between them.

Since their meeting in Transport, Gianni's attitude toward her had been aloof. No flicker of the heat and passion from last night. Gone was the man who had danced with her, kissed her, held her.

"Our client is Vittorio Felipe Vasquez." Anika recited the details from the mission briefing for the third time. "He controls a paramilitary force that oversees the usual gamut of illegal activities—drugs, prostitution, gambling, arms dealing. All concentrated in the southern Pacific lowlands."

So far, the El Salvadoran government had been unsuccessful in stopping Vasquez's crimes and bringing him to justice. The best it had been able to do was to plant an operative inside his operations to monitor his next moves.

It had taken years, but the operative had finally entered Vasquez's inner circle and earned the leader's confidence. That's how the government had learned of Vasquez's desire to extend his operations north, all the way to the Guatemalan border. To do so, he had to eliminate a rival, Isobela Carmen Tobar, who happened to be his ex-lover. She was this mission's target.

Vasquez had decided to hire a non-local assassin to carry out the hit. He wanted expertise and, more importantly, neutrality. He was concerned Tobar might catch wind of his plan and try to turn a local with the promise of their own territory as a reward. Vasquez preferred somebody with no interest in El Salvador, with only money as a motivation. He'd tasked the government mole inside his organization to identify the best person for the job.

This was where U.N.I.T. 605 entered the picture. The El Salvadorian government retained the agency to eliminate both Vasquez *and* Tobar, and shut down their unlawful operations so it could restore law and order to the territory now under their control. The agency offered to provide a husband-and-wife assassination team to carry out the first critical step of the assignment.

The plan was to kill Tobar, provide undeniable proof of her death to Vasquez (most likely, her decapitated head), then kidnap Vasquez and insert Agent Santos in his place. U.N.I.T. needed Vasquez alive so he could provide intel about the workings of his organization that could be fed to Santos. Agent Santos had completed the medical procedures to look, sound, and walk like Vasquez, even down to the limp in his right leg. Masquerading as the ruthless jefe and working in concert with the government operative, Santos would dismantle the paramilitary organization and give back control of the now-consolidated territory to the El Salvadoran government. As soon as the government had reasserted its authority, Agent Santos would be extracted and the real Vasquez would be returned to the country for trial and, in all likelihood, execution.

Once U.N.I.T's plan was approved by the government, a fee of twenty million dollars was paid into the agency's bank account. The mole recommended the American born-and-bred "Bianchis," and provided the necessary documentation—courtesy of the tech ops team at U.N.I.T.—as proof of their skill, including past hits.

Vasquez accepted the mole's recommendation to hire the Bianchis and approved the transfer of one-half of their fee—five million dollars—into a Swiss bank account. The money was sitting there now, waiting until the mission was complete, when it would be transferred again, this time into the agency's account as final payment for services rendered.

Anika glanced over at Gianni, his still profile a statue carved from fine Italian marble. "Can I ask you a question?"

He nodded, not turning his head.

"Do you know what the weather was on our wedding day?"

"What?" Gianni's head swung toward her, his eyes dark and intense.

"I mean," Anika said, running her tongue across her upper lip in a nervous gesture, "on Antonio and Lena's wedding day. There was nothing about the weather in the mission profile. I thought it might come up in conversation. You know, along with being asked about our... *their* previous assignments."

"It's best not to invent new information about backstories," Gianni said. "Use the data ops has provided."

Though his voice was dispassionate, or maybe because of it, irritation pricked the back of Anika's neck. They were supposed to be a team on this mission.

"I'm not *inventing* anything," she said. "I was trained that small details can make a cover more convincing. And according to ops, Antonio and Lena were married in Sonoma, California North on August twenty-eighth, twenty-sixty. I think most couples would remember the weather on their wedding day. So I looked it up. It was hot. Fried-tofu-on-sidewalk hot. Thirty-six degrees Celsius in the morning climbing ten more degrees before midday." Still meeting Gianni's gaze, Anika lifted her chin. "After the ceremony, the newlyweds ate ice cream."

A glimmer lit Gianni's eyes and the lines around his mouth softened. "What flavor? Nocciola?"

"Hazelnut?" Anika crinkled her nose. "I'd prefer chocolate."

"A mixed cup, then."

"Shared?"

"Of course, tesoro."

"Tesoro. That's Italian for treasure," Anika said.

"Yes. Antonio's endearment for Lena."

"That's not in the profile."

"No, but it is a small detail. Unless you disagree, or prefer something else?"

"'Tesoro' is fine." Even though it was her cover's nickname, the endearment from Gianni's lips, his tongue rolling out the "r," sparked a glow in Anika's chest that radiated to her limbs. "And I'll call you 'Nino,' short for Antonio. Okay?"

Gianni nodded, a small smile playing across his mouth. "Anything else?"

The thaw in his behavior encouraged her. "The souvenir vid. Why didn't we have to make one?"

"We decided that Antonio and Lena are extremely cautious people. Given their line of work, it makes sense they would carry clean handhelds on every assignment. No contact information, no message history, no personal mementos. All that would be secured in their house, without risk of possible hacking and public exposure."

"Who's 'we'?"

"I discussed it with Second. She agreed with my thinking."

"When did you think of it?"

"Early this morning."

"So, after..." Anika trailed off, unable to complete the sentence. *After our first—no, third—time.*

Gianni nodded.

"Otherwise, last night wouldn't have happened? Unless," Anika said, emboldened by the warmth in his eyes, "you could no longer resist my charms?" She smiled at him, hoping he would match her flirtatious tone. Say something like, *From the moment I saw you, I've wanted you.*

Instead, Gianni's eyes hardened to stones. He leaned away from her. It was like a wall of bullet-proof glass had slammed between them. The swift change stilled the breath in her lungs.

"You realize this mission is dangerous, don't you?" His words penetrated the imaginary glass. "It's not a sim. The targets are real. The ammo is real. No ops support. You need to get your head in it. Forget about everything else."

An icicle of fear pricked a trail down Anika's back. Her pulse tapped a fast beat. "I understand," she said, a catch in her voice.

"Do you?" His eyes locked on hers as the muscle near his jaw flexed.

His handheld buzzed and he turned away from her to answer it. "Yes?" He stood up. "Yes, Second, we're on schedule." He walked toward the back of the plane and, when the call was over, sat down in the single seat across the aisle. Ignoring Anika, he studied his handheld.

She turned her head to look out the small window. Brilliant swaths of pink and magenta painted the sky above a floor of purple clouds. But she didn't see the beauty. She saw only the dark vacant eyes of the Serbian hostile she had killed. *I do understand.*

Chapter 14

"To success. *¡Salud!*" Vittorio Vasquez raised his wine glass in a toast.

"*¡Salud!*" Anika replied, her voice joining with Gianni's.

They were seated next to each other, with their host at the head of the dining table set with heavy china, gleaming silverware, and crystal goblets. Anika took a sip of the ruby-colored wine. An expensive vintage, it was a delicious blend of spicy and smooth. But the knowledge they were sharing a meal with a brutal criminal left a sour taste in her mouth. The only way to get rid of the taste was to complete the mission. She couldn't wait to do that.

After they had landed on a private airfield, Gianni and Anika were met by a driver who brought them to the estate about a hundred kilometers outside the coastal city of La Libertad. Per the mission profile, Santos had stayed with the jet. If all went according to plan, he would spend a boring couple of days and nights in the small jet until the hit was carried out. And if the plan went south, Anika and Gianni had an escape vehicle at the ready.

In the meantime, they were guests of a jefe del crimen with ambitions to spread his power and terror throughout the country. In person, Vasquez was more attractive than the images shown at the mission briefing. His dark eyes were deeply set in a square face framed by equally dark wavy hair. He looked older than thirty-two, the age stated in U.N.I.T.'s intel. The closely-cropped beard and long scar over his left eyebrow probably contributed to that impression, but more likely, his premature aging was due to a lifetime of chaos and bloodshed.

Anika had pored over his profile, forcing herself to study the horrific images of his victims—dismembered corpses, mutilated bodies, red-rimmed eyes of grieving mothers and wives, stunned gazes of children. *Orphans*, Anika thought, a potent mix of anger and sorrow swelling inside her. Who would care for them? Other family members? Or had they been sent to live in an orphanage, a cold institutional place like the one where she had grown up?

Tobar's profile wasn't that much different. Certainly no better. She was directly responsible for thirty-three deaths that they were aware of, only slightly fewer than Vasquez. Together, their foot soldiers had killed hundreds more. The two leaders embodied no-shades-of-gray *evil*. They deserved their fate. This mission synced with Anika's reasons for joining U.N.I.T. Besides giving her a place to belong, the agency also gave her a reason to belong, a chance to do good in the world. Eliminating these two monsters and stopping their illegal operations certainly qualified.

A young girl who looked about fifteen appeared through an arched doorway with plates of grilled bistec, rice, beans, and fried platanos. Eyes downcast, she moved in near-silence, her mid-length cotton dress swaying around her slender figure. After she had set a plate in front of each of them and refilled their wine glasses, she disappeared in the direction she had entered. Her presence reaffirmed Vasquez's lucrative successes. Over the past decades, human servers had become increasingly rare, mostly found in the homes of the ultra-wealthy.

I guess crime does pay, Anika thought. *Until it doesn't.* She was eager for the moment when Vasquez would face his reckoning.

"How did you two meet?" Vasquez asked. "I understand it was

through your work."

Here we go. Anika's mind sharpened on the details from the mission briefing about the unusual circumstances of Lena and Antonio Bianchi's first meeting.

"You're referring to the job in Kurdistan," Nino replied. "I presume you've watched the videos, both the client referral and the real-time documentation of the hits?"

"Of course," Vasquez said, nodding. "I always questioned the official story as reported by the media. I was fascinated to learn the truth, to see the exact moment when the bullets struck their target, from the vantage point of the one who fired. *Two vantage points,* I should say. Both of yours. I was particularly intrigued by your client's decision to hire not one but two experts to dispose of the newly-elected president. How did he acquire the necessary funds, I wonder? From the Russians?"

"I didn't know at the time," Nino said. "I respect my clients' privacy. As long as they meet my financial requirements, I am satisfied. But not Lena."

Lena smiled at Nino. "You know me so well, sweetheart." She glanced at Vasquez. "I like to know who's bankrolling my clients. The Russians did give Dost the money."

The client under discussion, Rafiq Dost, was the well-known leader of Kurdish dissidents. He had campaigned unsuccessfully for the presidency. In the aftermath of his loss, Dost turned to the Russian government for help. He asked for money to hire a pair of assassins, twin brothers, to kill the president-elect. In exchange, he offered the Russians favorable access to his country's natural resources after his presumed rise to power in the vacuum created by the assassination.

Only part of the plan worked. The president-elect was indeed assassinated, but Dost never gained the power he sought. Instead, the vice president-elect—now the default president-elect—hired U.N.I.T. 605 to hunt down the twin assassins and Dost. Once captured, the dissident leader was turned over to the new Kurdish government. At his trial, he claimed sole responsibility for the assassination in order to secure leniency for his fellow dissidents. The role of the Russians and the existence of the assassins were never publicly revealed. Dost was found guilty and hanged. But his capture, trial, and punishment all took place *after* his post-mission meeting with the assassins—who video-recorded a referral from every client as part of their fee.

U.N.I.T. acquired a trove of client referral and assassination videos when they captured the twin brothers, now serving several lifetimes of imprisonment in a secret location. The authentic videos from their many jobs, with only minor tweaks made by the tech ops team, had been a crucial resource in helping build credible covers for assassination missions, including this one. As far as Vasquez knew, Nino and Lena had been the ones to take out the Kurdish president, not the twin brothers.

"Where do your funds come from?" Lena asked Vasquez.

Anika forced herself to meet his gaze, especially when his pupils contracted to knife tips.

"My customers. Mostly Americans. Los Estados Unidos is still the biggest market for my...ah...type of goods and services."

Lena tilted her head in acknowledgment of the truth of his statement. Her fellow citizens did, indeed, provide a robust marketplace for Vasquez's illegal businesses.

"But back to Rafiq Dost for a moment longer. In his referral video, he said that he didn't tell either of you about hiring the other." Vasquez chuckled. "I imagine it was quite a surprise when you discovered the truth."

Nino took Lena's hand in his. "A lovely surprise," he said, smiling at her.

Anika returned the smile, pleased that she didn't overreact to his touch, unlike when they had first arrived at the estate. As soon as they exited the car and started walking toward the front door of the main house, Gianni had reached for her hand. She had started at the gesture of affection, given how cold and silent he had been during the last hours of the plane ride and the short drive to the residence. Gianni had spoken a low reprimand. "Work your cover."

Now, Lena squeezed his fingers. "Oh, Nino, you *say* it was a lovely surprise. But I recall a different reaction at the time."

Vasquez leaned forward in his seat, glancing between them. "Tell me."

"Nino perceived Dost's behavior as disrespectful," Lena said.

"It *was* disrespectful," Nino added.

"I think you made that clear when you tried to shoot him during the follow-up meeting."

"I would have done so *if* you hadn't drawn your own weapon on me."

"I needed to make sure Dost survived long enough to authorize the balance of my payment," Lena said.

"I was only aiming for his shoulder." Nino gave a lazy shrug. "He would have survived."

"Who hit the target?" Vasquez asked.

"We both did, of course," Lena said. "During the president-elect's inaugural speech to the nation. Nino and I had taken up different positions, calculated different angles for the kill shot. Our eyes met through our scopes. It was..." She paused for effect.

Nino raised her hand to his lips, his breath warm against her skin. "Magical," he said, finishing the sentence.

Goosebumps sprang along her bare arms. Out of the corner of her eye, she saw Vasquez take note of the spark that passed between them. She had responded as Anika, but it worked for her cover as well.

"But which one of you made the kill shot?" Vasquez's eyes shone with disturbing curiosity.

Anika's stomach clenched. She dropped his gaze to hide her disgust.

"That depends." Gianni kept hold of her hand, his touch a buffer against the client's cold-bloodedness.

"On what?" Vasquez's eyebrow quirked up, creating a crease in his scar.

"On the current year. Odd years, I made the fatal shot. Even years, Lena did."

"You alternate taking credit?" Vasquez asked, both brows lifting.

"We agreed it was best for each other's well-being," Lena replied. "We even formalized the agreement in our wedding vows."

Vasquez threw back his head and laughed, then raised his glass. "You two are quite the pair. I almost feel sorry for anyone who becomes your target."

Anika raised her glass to hide the smile that tugged at her lips. This time, the wine went down smoothly. No sour aftertaste.

"You married soon after that meeting, as I recall," Vasquez said. "Wasn't it only four weeks?"

"Six," Nino replied. "I would have preferred sooner, but Lena made me wait, clever woman that she is."

"Good things come to those who wait." Lena leaned toward Nino and pressed her lips against his temple. "Isn't that right, darling?"

"I hope the fog didn't spoil your special day," Vasquez said. "I always thought San Francisco would be the perfect city if not for the fog, the earthquakes, and the smoke from the wildfires. Oh, and the decaying sea wall."

A trill of satisfaction sang through Anika. She had been right to research the weather as part of their aliases' background. A smile tugged at the corners of her mouth. "Nothing would have spoiled our wedding day." She sat back in her chair and looked at Vasquez, whose gaze was a bird of prey, vigilant for any sign of weakness. "We were married in Sonoma, a small town seventy-six kilometers north of San Francisco. And the weather was perfect."

"If you enjoy heat," Nino added. "Forty-six degrees before noon."

"It gave us an excuse to eat ice cream after the ceremony."

Gianni turned his head toward her, a spark of shared memory lighting his eyes. "Cioccolato e nocciola."

"You remember," Lena said.

"Of course, tesoro."

For the rest of the dinner, Vasquez asked about the Bianchis' other assignments. Clearly, he had conducted his own intelligence into their backgrounds—or at least, the intelligence U.N.I.T. had fabricated for their covers. He interspersed open-ended questions with more directed ones, sprinkling in the occasional false detail that they corrected. Although his posture was relaxed, with one arm slung across the back of his chair, Vasquez's gaze remained alert, wary.

Lena and Nino took turns speaking.

At first, Anika rushed Lena's words, like a debriefing she wanted to wrap up in a hurry. But Gianni slowed her down with small interruptions and gentle knee-nudges under the table. Soon, their responses took on an easy, intimate rhythm.

Nino waited until the server had removed the last of their plates before he steered the conversation back to the reason they were here. "When can we review the floor plans, alarm codes, security team details?"

Highly secretive, Vasquez had refused to provide details of Tobar's location, security protocols, or itinerary until they were face-to-face.

"Sí, sí, I have all of that ready. You can conduct your review tomorrow." Vasquez waved his hand in the air as if dispelling an unpleasant odor. "Also, I am returning your handhelds to you." He set the devices, confiscated as soon as they had arrived at the residence, on the table. "Thank you for understanding. The head of my security team is very cautious. As you said, the devices are clean. Nothing on them. Not even a souvenir vid."

The questioning tone in his voice made Anika wonder if it had been a mistake to omit all details from their covers' lives.

"We are every bit as cautious as your head of security," Nino said. "And thank *you* for your understanding."

A moment of silence stretched into long, uncomfortable seconds. Anika's breath grew shallow.

Vasquez smiled and broke the tension. "De nada." Girlish voices sounded from the hallway. He turned his head in that direction, saying, "Ah, here they are."

Two young women, their arms linked, sauntered into the dining room. They were tall and striking, with impossibly elongated torsos and limbs. They reminded Anika of the paintings by Amedeo Clemente Modigliani, the Italian artist she had admired in her high school art class. If Modigliani had painted super models. The women's summer-white sheath dresses were the length of a nanometer and afforded the viewer an impressive length of tanned legs. With enormous dark eyes, sky-high cheekbones, straight noses, and full lips, they were mirror images of each other, except for their hair color: one blond, one brunette.

"Suzette, Claudette, come meet our guests."

They approached Vasquez at the head of the table and perched on the arms of his chair, one on either side, human bookends. The blond draped her slender arm around the back of his neck. He ran a street-toughened hand from the brunette's knee up her bare thigh. The women's eyes were glassy and vacant. They didn't say a word.

Vasquez looked at Nino. "French imports. From Paris. Muy guapas, ¿no?"

Nino glanced around the room, appraising the handsome decor of gray and brown stone walls, wooden beams, and bronze statues of warriors. He lifted his wineglass. "You have excellent taste. In everything."

Vasquez bowed his head in silent appreciation. "The chicas and I usually take a swim after dinner. Join us. There are extra swimsuits in the cabana, if you feel the need." His gaze crawled across Lena's eyes, lips, breasts. Stopped. "We prefer to go without."

Anika pressed back into her chair, trying to create distance from their host. She didn't know how to respond. The invitation, more a command, repelled her. The look in Vasquez's eyes even more so. She wanted to tell him to go to hell. But maybe his invitation was a test. What would Lena do? She steeled herself to say "yes" and pushed her chair away from the table.

Nino stood. "Perhaps we'll join you in a bit." He took Lena's hand and helped her up. "After we've had time to digest your delicious meal."

Vasquez gaze switched to Nino. The two men remained motionless, each waiting for the other to break the silence. "As you wish." Vasquez dipped his head. Anika released a quiet breath of relief. "There's rum, mezcal, whiskey in the bar in the living room. Also, a one-hundred-year-old cognac that is almost worth its outrageous price. Please feel free to help yourselves."

"Thank you."

Nino and Lena walked down a set of shallow stairs that led into an adjacent room. The stone wall along one side projected rotating scenes of the kind of naturescapes now mostly found only in a virtual world—open fields of wildflowers, long stretches of beaches, snow-capped tops of mountains. At the room's far end, flames leapt in a giant fireplace. The fire was for atmosphere only as the breeze blowing in from the open windows was mild. Even in December, the daily temperatures here were noticeably warmer than New Angeles. That would make their nighttime assault on the target's residence easier. No need for cold weather gear.

Nino filled a snifter with the expensive cognac and offered it to Lena.

Anika took a cautious sip. Though she had been exposed to a wide variety of beers, wines, liquors, and rec-drugs in her training, she hadn't managed to develop a taste for cognac, no matter how expensive it was. The liquid created a trail of dying embers inside her mouth and down her throat.

"Do you like it?" Gianni asked.

Anika shook her head.

"May I?" He swirled the liquid in the bowl of the glass before sampling it. "Hmmm. A predominant blend of chocolate, toffee, and..." He took another sip.

"Clove," Anika said.

"I agree." Gianni lifted a brow. "Impressive."

A warm glow suffused her.

Rhythmic sounds of guitars, flutes, harmonicas, and drums floated through the room, while shouts of laughter and water splashing came from outside.

Nino wrapped one arm around her waist and swayed to the music. His touch magnified the glow from the alcohol. "You saw the cams?" Gianni asked, his mouth brushing against her ear.

Anika recoiled at the coolness in his voice. Such a contrast from the heat of his body. The glow inside her dissipated. While she hadn't seen any surveillance cameras in this room yet, based on what she had seen of the house so far, the cameras were everywhere. She gave a tiny nod.

Lena cupped the back of Nino's neck and pulled him in for an open-mouthed kiss.

They danced away from the bar, moving in time with the pulsing rhythm.

"More?" Nino held up the glass.

Anika shook her head. It was hard enough to keep her mind on why they were here while Gianni's nearness continued to send tiny shockwaves through her. More alcohol would make it impossible.

Nino pressed his lips against the curve in her neck.

Goosebumps bubbled up on her skin. Anika ignored them, while Lena sought out his mouth again. If this was a test of her ability to maintain her cover, she was damn well going to ace it.

"You were right," Gianni whispered, his breath warm on her lips.

"About researching the weather on our wedding day. Good work." His gaze poured into her.

The unexpected praise fed oxygen to the spark between them. She tilted her head and pursed her lips in invitation. Gianni—or maybe Nino—leaned forward in acceptance.

"¿Quieres bailar conmigo?" The blond woman, still wearing her dress, but no shoes, appeared at their side.

Anika pulled away from Gianni and cursed the interruption in silence.

"I mean," the woman said, reverting to English, "you want dance... with me?"

"No, he doesn't." Frustration sizzled in Anika. She wanted, if only for a moment longer, to stay connected with the man inside the operative, the one who had made love to her last night. This stoned-out woman was disturbing that fragile bond. What would Lena do? Play the strong-willed, possessive wife, maybe. She pushed in front of the woman. "Step away from my *husband*."

The woman bit down on her lip and glanced back over her shoulder, before returning her gaze to Gianni. "Vittorio wants me...I give you... good time."

"I'm all the good time he needs, or wants." Lena pressed close to Nino, stroked his cheek. "Isn't that right, darling?"

"Yes, tesoro." Nino took Lena's hand and kissed it. "Don't worry." He directed his words to the woman, who had clasped her arms across her chest and was shifting from one foot to the other. "I will be sure to let Señor Vasquez know how much I appreciate his invitation."

Nino slid his arm around Lena's waist and guided her away from the woman toward the crackling fire. They continued to hold each other, as if lost in their own private world, even after the music ended. Keeping his lips near her ear, Gianni whispered, "I'm going to take a walk around the property and conduct more surveillance."

"I'll come with you."

94

"You take the house. Cover as much as you can without arousing suspicion. I expect Vasquez will want to enjoy a cigar after his swim. I'll join him. Learn what I can about his operations."

"I thought we were a team on this assignment."

"We each have our roles to play. Vasquez will be more open without a beautiful woman around to try and impress."

Lena brushed her hand across his cheek. "Just make sure a cigar is all you enjoy with him," she said, her voice knife-tip sharp.

Nino pressed his lips to her forehead. "Don't wait up for me."

Oh, but I will, Anika thought. Nodding, Lena agreed.

Chapter 15

S alt from the sea water flecked the air around Anika. It swirled through her nostrils and settled at the back of her throat. She sat in a forward position on the bench seat of the inflatable ocean raft, helmed by Gianni, as it bounced across the waves. Clouds drifted past a half moon, providing brief intermittent views of the passing coastline.

They were en route to Isobela Tobar's home, ninety-five kilometers up the coast. She lived in a plexisteel-and-glass structure set high on a cliff overlooking the Pacific Ocean. While Anika and Gianni would have preferred to intercept her during a drug or arms run, preferably near one of Vasquez's controlled borders, Tobar hadn't been spotted outside of her residence in months. They had no choice but to risk a home assault.

She and Gianni had spent the previous day in full prep mode. In the morning, they had studied the logistical details and determined a plan of attack. The afternoon had been devoted to tactical drills. Vasquez's technology was a crude mimicking of the target's house and grounds, including ingress routes, floor layouts, and security team configs, but by day's end Anika felt she had mastered the basic entry and take-down approach. Training and instinct would have to handle any surprises along the way.

Anika flexed her right wrist, testing it. No twinges. *Good.* The pain meds were still working. Yesterday's multiple climbs had left her wrist aching. But she'd needed practice with the gloves—they were the only things that would keep her from falling off the cliff wall to certain death. She and Gianni had argued about who would handle the approach via the cliff wall. Even though the tech team had told them the gloves would only support Anika's body weight, Gianni had insisted on trying them out. After his third unsuccessful attempt to scale a wall on Vasquez's estate, Gianni had conceded she would take the wall, while he used the elevator.

As the raft sped forward, Anika rehearsed the proper motions to work the gloves: a firm open-handed slap against the climbing surface, followed by a rolling peel from the palm's heel up to the fingertips.

Watching her from the bench directly opposite was Vasquez, his presence a reminder that missions sometimes required last-minute adjustments. After another delicious dinner, he had announced his intention to join the mission. "You two secure the target," he had said. "But I want to kill the bitch myself."

Alarms bells had blared in Anika's head. Having Vasquez as a ride-along was not part of their plan.

Before she could open her mouth to veto the idea, Nino spoke up. "Understood."

Anika didn't understand. And Lena sure as hell didn't. "It's too late for changes now," she said. "We've only prepped for a two-man scenario."

"From where I sit, there *are* only two men in the scenario." Vasquez subjected her to another slithery gaze.

Anika's anxiety morphed into Lena's anger. She gripped the chair's arms and prepared for battle.

From underneath the table, Gianni pressed his leg against hers in silent warning. "We'll make the necessary modifications. But we'll need more of your men on the ground, as distractions."

"And we'll need more compensation," Lena said. "Change fees. As stipulated in our contract."

"Contract?" Vasquez's eyebrows pinched together.

Oh, shit, Anika thought, realizing her mistake. She didn't actually know if there was a contract—the mission profile hadn't mentioned one. Did assassins use them?

"Our contracts are verbal," Nino added. "A simple 'yes' will do."

"How much more?" Vasquez asked.

"Twenty-five percent." Lena relaxed back in her chair.

"Ten."

"Twenty-two." Lena lifted her glass of wine.

"Twelve." Vasquez leaned toward her, reaching for her glass with his own. "I'm providing more manpower."

"True." Lena pulled back just as their glasses were about to touch. "Twenty and a quarter." She threw in a flirtatious smile for good measure.

"Muy bien." Their glasses touched. The chime of expensive glassware sounded between them.

On the way back to their room, Gianni had dipped his head away from direct view of the hallway cams, and murmured, "Get ready."

Nino grabbed Lena's arm in anger. "You shouldn't have told Vasquez he couldn't come on the mission once I agreed. *Never* contradict me in front of a client."

Lena jerked her arm out of Nino's grasp. "You shouldn't have agreed without consulting me."

"And stop flirting with him. It's unprofessional."

"I was *negotiating.* It's extremely professional. And, at twenty and a quarter percent, extremely lucrative." Lena stopped in her tracks. "And since you brought up flirting, where were *you* last night?"

"What are you talking about?" Nino's eyes narrowed and shot sparks at her.

Anika rocked back on her heels, but Lena pressed ahead. "You never came to bed. Not ours, anyway. Maybe Claudette's? Or Suzette's? Or both?" The questions came fast and hard from Lena, even though Anika already knew the answer was no. Gianni had told her so earlier this afternoon, before he had suggested this mock-fight.

Nino unleashed an angry stream of Italian.

While Anika's brain translated key words—crazy woman...cigar... marriage vows...ridiculous...enough—Lena crossed her arms and waited.

When silence again filled the air between them, Anika switched subjects to escalate the fight. Drawing from her agency training, she chose a typical area of conflict between married people. "And this year," she said, "we're going to *my* mother's for the holidays. I've already made the reservations."

Nino threw up his hands and stalked off.

Lena waited until he had disappeared around the corner.

Then, for the benefit of the cams, Anika sighed out loud. "Oh, Nino, so predictable. Always a fight so close to an assignment." She hugged her arms around her waist. "Anything to avoid sleeping with your wife and losing focus on the job. Then again, you always make it up to me afterward."

Although the mock fight had been orchestrated for the surveillance cameras, the excuse it provided for Nino and Lena to sleep in separate rooms again was really for Gianni and Anika's benefit. Gianni had been the one to suggest it as they were enjoying refreshments on the balcony outside their room after a morning of mission prep.

They were looking out over the pool and garden beyond, their backs to the room and to the surveillance cams in the upper corners. Anika tipped her face to the afternoon sun, enjoying a rare moment of peace and stillness. They had spent an intense morning going over and over the assault plan, reviewing tactics, making adjustments, testing the equipment. Anika was tired, but also exhilarated. She and Gianni had developed a rhythm of working together like fluid dance partners. She was more confident than ever of the mission's success.

"You've noted the surveillance cams?" Gianni asked.

"Yes, they're everywhere. Two out here. Four in the room behind us, one in each corner. More in the bathroom," Anika replied.

"The ones in our room provide unobstructed views of the bed."

Anika's stomach suddenly jittered. "I noticed." She had been so pre-occupied with the logistical and physical preparations for tomorrow's assault on Tobar's residence that she had forgotten about the coming night and sharing a bed with Gianni as his pretend-wife.

Gianni placed his hand on hers. "I'd prefer not to perform for Vasquez's security team."

Her pulse quickened at his touch. "We could just...sleep?" she asked, although she didn't think she would be able to fall asleep with him lying next to her.

His lips quirked. "That would require too much self-discipline on my part."

"Is that why you didn't sleep in here last night?"

He nodded.

"Where did you sleep?"

"In a different guest room. Vasquez told Suzette to join me."

Anika's stomach dropped. She pulled her hand away. "The blond? You slept with her?" Hurt and anger fused into a fireball in her chest. To calm down, she told herself it wasn't Gianni who had slept with Suzette. It was *Nino*. Gianni was only acting the part. Still, the image of two pairs of naked arms and legs tangled together was like a painful bruise in her mind.

"No, I didn't sleep with her." Gianni reached over to brush a lock of hair off Anika's face. His fingers lingered against her cheek. "I told her I was touched by Vasquez's generosity, but that I am in love with my wife. I have no need or want of another woman."

A quenching relief rushed through Anika. *He hadn't slept with her.* Or, rather, he *had* slept with her. But only that. Nothing more. "I'm glad." She took a beat to steady herself. "What did Suzette say?"

"Honestly, she seemed relieved. And quite happy just to go to sleep."

Anika felt a twinge of sympathy. Suzette's reaction was understandable. She and Claudette were clearly under Vasquez's control and compelled to do whatever he asked. Gianni's disinterest in sleeping with her had probably seemed like an unexpected gift. Her relief made complete sense.

Gianni took Anika's hand in his, lifted her palm to his mouth, and planted a kiss there. Tiny sparks raced down her arm and exploded in her chest. "About tonight, then."

She was having second thoughts about staying in separate rooms again. Maybe they could disable the cameras or find a hidden nook where they wouldn't be seen or...

That's when Gianni had suggested that Nino stage a fight. And have Lena explain it as typical behavior on his part the night before an assignment.

Anika had invented the bit about Nino always making it up to Lena afterward.

As the moon peeped out from the clouds, Vasquez pointed to a silhouette of a house at the edge of a cliff. "There," he said.

Gianni reduced speed and angled the raft toward a small cove where they would beach. When they reached shallow water, Gianni cut the motor.

The knots in Anika's stomach tightened.

Vasquez checked his handheld. "Ninety seconds until the next security cam sweep."

Anika fired the turbo-harpoon at the far cliff wall that semi-circled the cove. The penetration point bit into the rock. She powered up the weapon. The hunting line retracted and pulled the raft onto the sand.

"Forty seconds," Vasquez said.

The three of them debarked. While Vasquez continued the countdown, Gianni deflated the raft and Anika set up a chameleon screen with side and overhead panels two meters' distance from the cliff's face. Like the animal after which the agency's tech team had named their invention, the screen's material changed to resemble a rock's coloring and texture. The camera's eye would only see it as an extension of the cliff wall.

The three of them stood in a tight formation in the space between the wall and the screen.

"Ten seconds to spare." Vasquez smiled his satisfaction.

The new plan hadn't required major changes to the original one. In some ways, Vasquez's desire to kill Tobar himself simplified things. Anika and Gianni had worked out the details that morning and gotten Vasquez's approval. Then they contacted Agent Santos in secret to bring him up to speed.

Anika and Gianni would still be the ones to breach Tobar's residence and isolate her inside. Vasquez would then join them. While his attention was focused on killing Tobar, Anika and Gianni would be focused on their double cross. As soon as Tobar was dead, they would sedate Vasquez, abduct him, and return to the cove, where they would rendezvous with Santos. There, the operatives would switch watercraft. Anika and Gianni would return to the hover plane with the real Vasquez while Santos would return to Vasquez's compound and feign victory at having taken down his fiercest rival himself. Then, Santos-as-Vasquez would start work on his mission of dismantling the illegal operations of Vittorio Vasquez and Isobela Tobar.

"The elevator to the house is along this wall?" Gianni, pointing north, asked Vasquez.

"Sí, four hundred meters," Vasquez said.

"And the code?"

"It resets every two minutes. When you're ready, I'll give you the next one in the sequence."

"Okay," Gianni said. "Tell your men to start."

Vasquez spoke into his handheld and gave commands for the frontal and rooftop assaults.

Soon, Anika heard a low-pitched hum. The swarm of laser-firing micro-drones was approaching. The air assault was strictly diversionary. The micro-drones would swoop and swerve above the roof to draw the attention of Tobar's guards and the anti-aircraft weapons. As the humming sound of the swarm grew louder, the peaceful lapping of ocean waves mixed with the staccato burst of gunfire.

While her location blocked any sounds of gunfire from the front of the house, Anika imagined that diversionary assault had also begun.

The real assault, from the sea—the most difficult and, therefore, the least expected—was the one she and Gianni were about to execute.

Chapter 16

"Review the sequence," Gianni instructed her.

"I start the climb to the lowest level, Tobar's bedroom suite," Anika said. "Eighteen seconds out, I give the go-ahead. You start up in the elevator tube. I finish the climb, plant the explosive on the window, retreat outside the blast zone. Wait for your signal. When it comes, I detonate the explosive to distract the security detail. Elevator door opens. You engage the hostiles. I climb back up and secure the target."

"Then you send the elevator back for me," Vasquez said. "I join you and take out the puta." He clapped his hands together and a smile spread across his face.

Anika's lips tightened in disgust. "Yes," she said. "For an additional twenty and a quarter percent."

Vasquez's smile faded, but he didn't contradict her.

Anika shed her outerwear to reveal a unisuit molded to her body. She wound her single long braid into a tight circle and pinned it to her head. From her kit bag, she withdrew a utility belt, mini-explosive, hand laser, and night patches. She slung the patches around her neck, strapped on the belt, secured the explosive, and holstered the laser. Lastly, she removed the electro-adhesive gloves and toe tips.

"You're sure there are no cams covering the cliff face?" she asked

Vasquez.

"I'm sure," he replied.

"If you're wrong, and I'm discovered, you'll never make it back alive. Nino will see to that."

"Don't worry. I want this as much as you do."

I doubt that, Anika thought. *You want to gain more power. I want to prove myself in the world's toughest counterterrorist organization.*

Gianni positioned a comm device in her ear and smoothed back a loose hair from her face. Her skin tingled from his touch. Without thinking, she leaned in for a kiss. *This could be our last time.* At the unbidden thought, her lips clung to his in a moment of desire and dread. *Please don't let this be our last time.*

"If I had doubts you two were lovers," Vasquez said, "and given your sleeping arrangements the last two nights, I did have doubts, that kiss erased them. *¡Dios mio!* I can feel the heat from here."

Anika glared at Vasquez. Her hand itched for the laser. *I'd like to give you heat.* That moment was coming, she reminded herself. A moment of justice, of payback for his crimes.

Gianni turned her face back toward his. "Focus," he whispered.

She looked up. 230 meters. Cakewalk. If she were a Salvadoran yellow-headed gecko. She took in a belly breath, let it stream out. Powered on the gloves and toe tips. "See you up there."

Anika extended her arms and slapped her hands against the cliff wall. The glove's adhesive material suctioned her palms and outspread fingers to the rocky surface. She bent her right leg, pressed the toe tip into the wall and felt the adhesive material grab hold. She pushed up and planted her left toe tip. Peeled her right hand away, from heel to fingertips, as she had practiced the day before. Smacked it farther up the wall. Did the same with her left hand. Then, right leg, left leg. Over and over.

Soon, the gentle *thumpf* of the ocean waves receded. There was only the thud of her pulse, the in-out of her breath, the slap-kick-push-pull of her limbs.

Eleven moves up, as she straightened her right leg, her foot slipped. Pebbles rattled down the cliff wall. Her heart rocketed into her throat. A gasp escaped her. Her hands clawed at their holds. The gloves loosened. The only secure hold was her left toe. *Shitshitshit.* Her body fell backward, but she managed to catch herself at the last minute, flinging out her arms and flattening her hands against the wall. She kicked her right toe into a different section. Both hands and toes sucked in tight against the rocky surface.

"Report." Gianni's voice sounded a million meters away.

Anika gulped in deep breaths of the sweet night air.

"Report status. Over." His voice vibrated.

She rubbed her sweat-slicked face against the sleeve of her unisuit. "Estimate forty-six meters to bedroom level. The gear doesn't work well on loose pebbled surfaces. I just learned that. I'll make sure to tell the—" Anika cut herself off. She had almost said "geek-boys." But Lena Bianchi wouldn't use that term. "...tell the supplier. Over."

"Good idea," Gianni said, his tone back to normal. "When we get back home. Over."

Home. She started to climb again. Was that Gianni or Nino talking? Did Gianni think of the agency as his home? Did she?

"Eighteen seconds out," she said. "Do you copy?"

"Copy that. Ascending in elevator. Over."

"Copy. Moving to bedroom window. Over."

Anika continued her crawl toward the large pane of reinforced glass that rang the length of the bedroom. A warm light glowed from within. As she grew closer, the percussive staccato of gunfire from the rooftop grew louder. The diversionary assault was still in progress.

She completed one final vertical push and stopped. "In position to set the explosive. Over."

"Copy. I'm in the elevator. Proceed. Over."

"Copy that." Clinging to the rock wall with both toes and her left hand, Anika peeled away her right hand and removed the puck-sized device from her utility belt. Reaching up, she attached it to the window's outside corner, then climbed back down the cliff until she was outside the blast radius. "Explosive in place. Awaiting your signal. Over."

"Copy that. Stand by. Over."

She imagined the scene inside the bedroom. Heavily armed guards surrounding the door of the single-person elevator tube, waiting with coiled patience for its arrival, waiting to unleash lethal blasts of laser fire, or maybe rounds of gunfire, on whoever was inside.

Her heart squeezed in fear. She prayed Gianni's magnetic harness attaching him to the elevator's interior ceiling would give him the necessary cover in those first critical seconds between the guards being distracted by the explosion and redirecting their attention—and firepower—to the elevator.

"Detonate," Gianni said.

Anika pushed the green button and hugged the cliff face. A deep-throated boom followed. Then a high-pitched tinkle of falling glass shards. The cliff moved, as if shaken by a giant. Short bursts of gunfire, *prll-prll-prll*, gave way to agonized cries.

Anika scrambled up. *Please be alive.* As she neared the blown-out window, she heard a strange command from Gianni. "Anika, hold your fire."

Why had he given her away? And why use her real name?

An even stranger sound came from the room. It was so unexpected that it took Anika a moment to place it. Piercing cries. No, not just cries. Howls. Wails.

A baby?

Chapter 17

Anika clung to the cliff wall and peered inside.

Three guards were down, limbs splayed, killed by the explosive. Regret twisted in her, but she shut it down. She couldn't afford to lose focus. She couldn't afford to be distracted from the mission. She chose to see the dead men as the killers they had been. More bad guys taken out of this world.

Gianni, the harness still strapped around his torso, stood in the middle of the room at the foot of a large bed. His hand gripped a laser, but it hung at his side. Sweat glistened on his face. Anika's throat constricted, like a cord pulling tight, at the sight of blood leaking from a wound in his left shoulder. His attention was focused on the far corner of the room.

A fourth man lay crumpled on the ground. From his position, it appeared he had been using his body as a shield for the woman huddled there now: Isobela Tobar.

Tobar cradled a wriggling shape in a blanket. Her dark hair fell in waves around her shoulders as she leaned over the bundle and murmured soothing sounds. She wore cotton drawstring pants and a tank top. Her bare feet were bleeding from the shattered pieces of glass that covered the floor like confetti.

"Come inside." Gianni spoke to Anika even while he kept his gaze on Tobar.

Anika pulled herself to the window ledge and dropped into the room. Glass crunched underfoot. "Are you okay?"

"Flesh wound. How was the climb?"

"Next time, I'll take the elevator."

A smile flickered across Gianni's face.

The tension in Anika's throat loosened and her next breath flowed in and out. "Why didn't Vasquez tell us," she said, gesturing toward Tobar, "about the baby?"

Tobar looked up. Her espresso-brown eyes burned. "He doesn't know. The only ones who knew are..." She looked at the men on the floor. "Dead."

So, this was why there had been no sightings of Tobar outside of her residence in recent months. She had been concealing a pregnancy and birth.

Anika stepped closer to Gianni. "This changes things," she said. "We can't ki—can't complete the mission now." No matter what terrible crimes the baby's mother had committed, Anika wasn't going to allow him—or her? —to become an orphan.

"New plan. We'll need your cooperation," Gianni said to Tobar.

"Why should I?" she sneered.

"So your child will live."

Tobar's eyes contracted to twin slits. Her lips drew a blade-thin line.

"Our organization is working with your government to close down your illegal operations," Gianni said. "Both yours and Vasquez's. We have arranged to insert a replacement for Vasquez. A man who looks and talks and moves like him. Initially, the plan was to kill you, kidnap Vasquez, and replace him with our man who, in your absence, would take over both operations. But now, you'll work with our man. We had anticipated a six-month timeframe. But it should go faster now, with your help. And our incentive."

"What incentive?" Tobar asked.

"To ensure your cooperation, we'll be keeping your child. Once the authorities are satisfied that the objective has been met, we'll return him."

Anika's stomach somersaulted. The idea of taking the newborn made her sick, but she knew Gianni was right. It was the only way to guarantee Tobar fulfilled her end of the deal.

"*Her*. She's my daughter." Tobar pulled the now-quiet bundle closer to her. "You're not taking her from me."

"It's either that, or go back to our original plan," Gianni said. "What do you think will happen to your daughter then?" Gianni's voice was gentle, but he kept a firm hold on his laser.

"We'll keep her safe," Anika said, her voice steady. "Just focus on the objective. The faster you meet it, the sooner you'll get your daughter back."

Fury smoldered behind the woman's tears. "You have children?"

Anika sipped in a deep breath, and shook her head. "I know what it's like to grow up without a mother. I won't let that happen to your child." She met the woman's fierce gaze. "As long as you do what's being asked."

The woman buried her face in the soft blanket and rocked her baby. It was hard to reconcile the woman's tenderness with the ruthlessness displayed in the gruesome images in her profile. The beheadings, the severed limbs, the charred bodies. While those images filled Anika with revulsion, the woman's behavior toward her child evoked a different response.

Anika looked away from a sight that threatened to split open heart-deep wounds. Her own mother had never held her like that. Or had she? Right before abandoning her in a monorail station?

"Any questions about the plan?" Gianni asked.

"What will happen to Vasquez? I hope you're going to kill the bastard."

"We're taking him back with us. Alive. He can provide intel about his operations, background, relationships that only he knows. And he can help verify information you may feed our man. For now, he's of greater value to us alive than dead. When the mission is over, we'll return him to the authorities here."

"That will also be my fate? To be given over to the authorities, or imprisoned for life, or executed?"

"You may be granted leniency in exchange for your help."

"If I help the authorities, I will be a dead woman in this country."

"There are other countries," Anika said.

The woman glanced back and forth between them. She exhaled a slow breath. "Very well. I accept your terms."

"I'll contact Vasquez," Gianni said. "Send down the elevator."

"Let me change first." Anika walked to a closet next to the elevator and pulled out a dark top and pants that resembled the clothing worn by the guards. While the pants stopped well short of her ankles, they fit over her hips and around her waist. She rolled up the legs of her unisuit so they were hidden underneath the pants fabric. "Call him," she said, then pressed the elevator button. She lay prone, facing the wall, next to one of the dead guards. Gritting her teeth, she placed the man's slack arm, still warm, over her head.

Minutes later, Vasquez strode from the bullet-pocked elevator cage. His gaze swept past the dead guards to focus on Tobar. She knelt on the floor, hands on her head, Gianni's laser trained on her. She had already settled her baby in the adjoining bathroom, surrounding her with towels and pillows in the tub. No sounds could be heard coming from there.

"Excelente," Vasquez said. "Hola, Isobela. I've dreamed of this moment for years. Although, in my dreams, tears streamed from your eyes and you begged for mercy."

"How's the scar?" Tobar asked.

Anika heard the taunt in her voice.

"No te preocupes," Vasquez said, shrugging. "A scratch compared to what I will do to your face when I carve on it."

Tobar spat on the floor.

Good for you, Anika thought. With Vasquez's attention still directed away from her, she rose to her feet in a swift, soundless movement.

Vasquez laughed. "Before I am through, you *will* beg." Looking at Gianni, he continued, "Worth every dollar I've paid. Even the surcharge for being able to do the kill myself. Which reminds me, where is your lovely *esposa*?"

Anika leveled her laser at Vasquez. "Behind you."

He looked back over his shoulder and saw the weapon. "What is this?" His brows pulled together, contorting the scar on his forehead.

"It's called a double cross. Call off your men. Tell them to pull back from the house and the rooftop."

Vasquez's eyes darkened. "Whatever she offered to pay you, I'll triple it."

Anika aimed at a point over his shoulder and fired. Her aim was off a fracture and the blast singed the top of his shoulder before it burned a hole in the wall behind him.

Vasquez cursed in pain. "*¡Puta!*"

"Make the calls."

Once Vasquez had given the commands, the staccato sound of gunfire from the roof receded, though it continued to echo in Anika's ears.

"What now?" he asked. "Are you going to kill me, or did she offer you extra to do the job herself?" Vasquez rocked forward on the balls of his feet and flexed his knees.

Anika gave no indication she had noticed the subtle change in his stance. "Neither," she said. "Unfortunately, you're more valuable to us alive than dead."

Something changed behind his eyes, as he realized what she meant. "Who is us?"

"You'll find out later. After your nap."

He leapt at her.

She sidestepped, fired, and stunned him into unconsciousness. "Sleep well, asshole." Glancing at Gianni, she said, "Thanks for letting me take him out."

"I wanted you to experience it for yourself."

"What?"

"A takedown for a worthy cause. That the agency is a force for justice. How does it feel?"

Anika looked down at Vasquez. "Pretty damn good."

Gianni tossed her his handheld. "Call Santos. Inform him of the new plan. Tell him to return to the hover plane, fly it here, mask up to disguise his resemblance to Vasquez and join us here. We'll take the plane back. With Vasquez and..." Gianni turned to Tobar. "What is your daughter's name?"

Tobar's eyes glistened with tears. "Lily Daniela." Her voice sounded like a prayer, like a plea.

Gianni nodded. "Contact your men on the roof. Tell them a plane will be arriving shortly. When it lands, they are to escort the pilot here. Get ready to meet your new partner."

"If any harm comes to my daughter, I will hunt you both down." Her eyes, dry now, raged at them.

Despite herself, fear prickled down Anika's back. In that look, she glimpsed the woman who had commanded a small army of dangerous criminals for almost a decade. She forced herself to hold the woman's gaze. "Understood."

Chapter 18

"Hey, did you just get back?" Mari walked toward Anika, who had cleared the final checkpoint in the corridor that led to Transport.

She and Gianni had returned minutes ago. The medic who met them took Tobar's infant daughter to Clinic while four guards escorted Vasquez, in restraints, to interrogation. Gianni told Anika to report to sub-level 1 for debriefing, then walked off in the same direction as the guards, leaving her to wonder when she would see him again.

Though she longed to spill out every twist and turn of the mission to her friend, Anika held back in deference to agency rules. "What happened to your hair?" She stared at her friend's shorn head, the bouncy curls replaced by brown fuzz only a few millimeters in length. "Did they make you cut it?"

"Nope." Mari ran her hand over her scalp, from front to back. "I asked someone in Makeup to do it. I wanted something different. Something that made me look badass. What do you think?"

To Anika, the absence of hair made her friend look younger, more vulnerable, her blue eyes even bigger in her round face. "You look fierce," she said. "I'd be scared if I ran into you in a dark alley."

"I can introduce you to the styling pro who did it. She can cut yours, too."

"No thanks. She'd have to tranq me and put me in restraints before I'd let her near my hair with a sharp instrument." The memory of forced haircuts at the orphanage still haunted Anika. Like the other girls in the orphanage, she had grown up with an ugly bowl-shaped cut that, along with a dirt-brown uniform, branded them kids of the government. Kids nobody wanted.

"Okay, okay, I get it. How'd the mission go?"

"Mari, you know I can't tell you."

"Just point. Thumb up or down?"

Anika pointed her thumb toward the ceiling.

Mari leaned in closer. "How was it to be with Gianni that whole time?"

Alarm pricked Anika. "How do you know he...we...he was on the team?"

"I saw you both heading to Transport three days ago. Figured you were on a two-person mission."

"Three." Anika thought about Diego Santos, the operative they had left behind. Would his mission be a success? Would Tobar cooperate and reunite with her daughter?

"So, how was it?" Mari prodded.

"It was fine."

"Fine? That's all I get? Come *on*. You gotta give me more than that."

"Gianni was focused on the mission. We both were."

"What about *after* the mission? On the ride back. You know," Mari said, her eyebrows peaking with curiosity, "when all that adrenaline is still revving your system?"

"We were babysitting a bad guy." *And an actual baby,* Anika thought, but didn't say it. "That was a system neutralizer."

Fortunately, Tobar's daughter had slept during the return flight. And Vasquez had been subdued with both drugs and body restraints. So, yes, Anika had enjoyed some alone time with Gianni. But not the kind Mari was talking about. After setting the plane on autopilot, he had taken the seat next to her and instructed the audio system to play Italian opera music. It was his favorite form of relaxation, he explained. Anika didn't especially like the music, but she did like sitting beside Gianni, their knees occasionally bumping, as they flew through the night sky.

His mood was lighter than it had been at the start of the mission. Lighter even since his return to the agency. She still wondered what had happened to him while he was gone. What had caused the dark shadows under his eyes and the grim lines around his mouth. She sensed an opening after the final strains of an aria had faded. But then his handheld buzzed and, after checking the caller ID, he walked to the front of the plane. When he returned, the shadows and lines were back. The call had shattered their renewed intimacy.

"You brought down a killer and not a scratch on you? You *are* a bad ass. Even with long hair." Mari tugged on the ends of Anika's hair, which hung past her shoulders.

"When's your mission?" Anika asked.

"Now. I've been working on my rappelling technique nonstop. Even in my sleep." Mari smiled, but Anika noted the flare of anxiety that darted through her friend's eyes.

"When are you back?"

"Six, maybe seven hours." A sigh escaped Mari. "I wish you were going, too."

"I could request it." Anika heard the reluctance in her own voice. All she wanted to do was spend some time in the relaxation tank and try to process the events and emotions of the past days.

"Nah," Mari said. "No time. Besides, you've already saved my ass in here. Twice."

"Yes, but the first time you were just a recruit."

"So were *you*. You were such an awesome recruit. The rest of us were so jealous, especially when you aced that training sim and earned the chance to go off-premise." Anika shrugged away the compliment. "It's time I saved my own life," Mari continued. "And the lives of some innocents. Wish me luck?"

Apprehension fluttered through Anika, dead leaves falling from a tree. She ran her hand across the top of Mari's head. The hair felt as soft as a baby duckling. "You don't need it. You've got training. You're ready."

Mari squared her shoulders. "Damn straight."

"Be safe," Anika whispered at her friend's departing back.

As she descended the stairs to the debriefing level and approached a room in the southwest wing, Anika replayed Gianni's words of advice. "Keep your statements simple," he had said, after their vehicle had rolled to a stop in an empty Transport bay. "Start with the mission's objectives. Then move on to actions. End on outcomes. Explain that some adjustments in the field were necessary and, ultimately, effective. Use your own words, but be sure to state that the mission was a success."

The set up in the room was similar to Anika's first debriefing. Four bare walls surrounded a metal chair that faced a small camera lens at eye level. No technician, no sensors. Just the camera's eye. Anika sat and steadied her breath. *Objectives, actions, outcomes. Objectives, actions, outcomes.*

The eye powered on and a computerized voice requested her name, tracking ID, and rank. After confirming her profile details, the voice asked her about the mission.

"The objectives were to extract Vasquez and insert Agent Santos in his place," Anika said.

"Incomplete," the voice responded.

Anika tried again. "The objectives were to extract Vittorio Vasquez and return him to U.N.I.T. alive. And to insert Agent Diego Santos in his place to work with local authorities shut down the illegal operations."

"Incomplete," the voice repeated. "State the third objective."

Anika knew what she had left out. To kill Tobar. Why was she reluctant to say that this objective had to be changed mid-mission? She still believed she was right to let Tobar live and Gianni had agreed with her; Santos had endorsed the change and they had Tobar's daughter in their custody to guarantee her mother's cooperation. So killing Tobar had no longer been required. But would U.N.I.T.'s leadership view it that way? Should she and Gianni have gotten prior approval before acting? He hadn't thought so and he was a Level 3. But Anika suddenly had doubts. Something about this sterile surveillance room set her on edge, made her question herself. It didn't help that she was still bothered by her failure in Belgrade. She had wanted this mission to be an indisputable win for the agency, and for her. Maybe she could ensure the agency viewed it just that way.

"The third objective," she said, "was to kill Isobela Tobar in order to expedite her organization's downfall. However, based on what Agent Brambilla and I encountered in the field, we needed to modify the kill order. We devised an alternative plan that would still produce the desired outcome." While she waited for the computer to process the statement, she forced her body to remain still. And to blink at a normal pace.

"Proceed."

The tightness in Anika's chest eased. The rest of her answers were succinct. When asked to sum up the mission, she answered, "It was a success."

The eye powered down. "Debriefing concluded."

Relief and satisfaction sluiced through her. She pushed up from the chair. Saying the words out loud made them feel real. The mission had succeeded. *She* had succeeded. Proved she belonged. She turned to exit the room when the door slid open. She froze. Resisted grabbing onto the chair back for support.

Second strode in on knife-sharp heels and platform soles that added significant height to her petite frame. "Take a seat."

Chapter 19

Anika wondered if the machine had detected something amiss in her debrief. Even though Gianni had told her to say the mission was a success, maybe it was too strong a statement given the improvised changes they had made. Maybe she should have made her summary more neutral. Stated that the mission objectives had been met. Left it at that.

Second positioned herself in front of Anika, her posture impeccable.

Anika forced herself to meet the second-in-command's gaze. The description Evan had given at Amnesia about Second's piercing blue eyes was exactly right. Anika felt those eyes could penetrate her skull and see her racing thoughts. Was it too late to change her final statement?

Second's dark blue suit jacket hugged her torso, like body armor. Her red-stained lips shone in the brightly lit room. Anika concentrated on those lips as they began to move. "I know this was your first extended undercover mission," Second said. "You performed well. Gianni, too. You made a good team. Congratulations."

Anika swallowed. Anxiety continued to shimmer through her. "Thank you." She sensed there was more.

Second extended her hand, palm up. In it lay a black handheld. "Do you recognize this?"

"It looks like a standard-issue handheld," Anika replied.

"It's *your* handheld."

"Mine?" Anika's brows creased. "I left mine in my apartment. Before leaving on the mission."

"Yes. We found it in our sweep while you were gone."

"You searched my apartment?"

"We conduct routine searches on all Level Ones' living quarters, both on- and off-premise."

In her mind, Anika scanned the interior of her apartment. Had she left anything out in the open that she shouldn't have? "I followed procedure in storing the handheld before I left."

"Yes, the team confirmed the handheld was secure. I wanted to ask you about a message in an encrypted file. Do you know the one I'm talking about?"

Of course she did. It was the message Gianni had left for her after their night together. The one he had told her to delete. Now, Second had seen it. Probably archived it in her profile. The knowledge made Anika's cheeks flame.

Second glanced at the screen. "Last night—"

"Yes, I know," Anika cut her off. *Last night was beyond all imaginings.*

"We know Brambilla visited your apartment the night before the mission went live. We presume the message is from him."

Am I in trouble? Is Gianni? "I'm not aware any agency rules have been broken."

"They haven't. Yet. We understand the biological need for sex, as a release or a distraction." Second's tone was clinical. It reminded Anika of the sex ed vids at the orphanage. She had yawned through those mandatory sessions. Now, it took all of her self-control to keep from squirming in her seat. "But we will not tolerate an emotional entanglement that interferes with mission performance. You were taught this as a recruit and I'm here to remind you how seriously we take that instruction. Understood?"

Anika wondered if Second had given the same message—*warning*—to Gianni. A rancid stew of anxiety, resentment and sadness bubbled inside her. Did this mean she had to choose between belonging and love? It was an impossible choice. She wanted both, but she knew Second wouldn't accept that answer, so she gave the only answer she could.

"I understand," she said.

"Good." Second gave her the handheld. "A piece of advice." Anika met the senior officer's gaze. "Don't conflate effective mission prep on Brambilla's part with...something else."

Second's parting words landed a body blow. Stunned, Anika sat in place until the clicking of high heels faded to silence.

Had Gianni's actions the night before the mission—the dancing, the champagne drinking, the lovemaking—all just been preparation for their cover? He had told her he didn't want their first time to be for a fake souvenir video. But maybe that, too, was part of his preparation. A planned seduction so she would do a better job. For the mission. But then why leave the message? More preparation for her alias as a beloved wife?

Anika powered on the handheld and jabbed the buttons until she found what she wanted. She punched delete and watched the message vanish. The gesture was futile. The words were already seared into her brain.

She spent the next several hours moving throughout the complex, trying to keep her mind and body busy. She started with a session in an immersion tank, but gave up after ten minutes. The tank was too quiet for her restless thoughts, even with the soothing sound of a steady breath piped into the space. Next, she visited the computer lab where she tested her responses to various mission scenarios. Then she wandered into the language lab and practiced her Mandarin and Farsi. She repeated key phrases—*on your knees, put down your weapons, I have the intel you want*—over and over until the computer gave her perfect scores. She walked up and down the rows of offices reserved for senior level operatives. Around every corner and in every new room, she found herself looking for Gianni. If she could talk to him, maybe she could discover for herself if Second was right. If their night together at her apartment had only been in service of the mission.

Anika entered the training facility. The air refresh system did not fully mask the potent mix of sweat, exertion, and tension absorbed by the gel mats, walls, training equipment. She scanned the zones nearest the entrance. Still no sign of Gianni. Disappointment pressed down on her, like a body-armor vest.

She moved into the cardio zone and stepped onto the gyro-track for forty-five minutes of interval training. She followed that with a sprint through the obstacle course and, after a fifteen-minute cool down, practice in a target chamber. There, she keyed in a mix of sims, alternating her shooting practice between right and left hands. No residual pain, not even a twinge, from her right wrist. Time and physical therapy had brought about a full recovery. She wiped the sweat from her face and arms and draped the microfiber towel around her neck while waiting for the computer to calculate her performance results. Ninety-nine percent accuracy. Four percentage points higher than all other operatives who had logged practice sessions this month. That brought a satisfied smile to her face.

Outside the target chamber, a pair of female recruits passed in front of her with their rappelling gear still on. God, they looked young in their matching tank tops and loose-fitting pants, hair pulled back from their tired faces. Both sported fading bruises on their bare arms, the signs of hand-to-hand training sessions. She remembered those long days and short nights of seminars, classes, workshops, tests. The anxiety of wondering if she would make the cut. The fear of being rejected, like all those times at the orphanage. The sight of the recruits' harnesses and grip gloves made her think of Mari. She wondered how the mission was going. Maybe she would grab some food in the dining annex and wait around to find out. She liked that idea more than returning to her apartment. Now that she knew about the agency's routine searches, the loft held less appeal, like a safe house under constant surveillance.

Anika's stomach rumbled, a reminder that her last proper meal had been the previous night at Vasquez's house. It was mind-bending to think of all that had happened in the intervening hours. Infiltration of Tobar's house, confrontation leading to a change in mission plans, exfiltration of Vasquez, return to agency, debriefing. The successful completion of her first extended cover mission. Even Second's warning about getting emotionally involved with Gianni, her insinuation that he had only seduced her for the purpose of mission prep, couldn't take that win from her. Her step lightened as she headed toward the exit at the front of the facility.

She noticed a small group of recruits in a half circle, their backs facing her, in the hand-to-hand training zone. Their bodies were clustered together and prevented her from seeing what was happening in front of them. She overheard someone say, "Look at her go. She's kicking his ass, too." Another said, "Who is she again?" A new voice spoke up. "New head of ops tech. Mega-hot. Name's Evelyn, I think."

Anika pushed between two sets of sweat-slicked shoulders and took in the scene before her. A man with a bloodied nose lay face up on the floor, unconscious. Another man lay on his back and absorbed blow after blow. On top of him sat Evan, one knee digging his groin, while she punched the life out of him. The man wasn't even trying to hit back, but only using his arms to shield his face from Evan's fists.

"Get a medic down here," Anika said to the girl on her right. "Now." She ran over to Evan, whose left eye was swollen shut. "Evan, that's enough."

The ops tech didn't seem to hear. She jerked her arm back for another blow.

Anika grabbed hold of Evan's arm. "Stop it. You've won."

Evan broke through the hold and landed another punch.

Her strength surprised Anika, given her small frame. Anika twirled her sweat towel into a makeshift blindfold and whipped it across Evan's eyes, holding on tight to the ends. She grabbed the back of Evan's collar and pulled her away.

Evan ripped off the towel and whirled to face Anika. Her lips snarled. She jabbed at Anika's throat.

Anika blocked her, and leapt back to create distance between them. "What are you doing?"

Evan charged.

Anika stopped her with a kick to the torso.

That did it. Evan slumped to her knees. Gasped for breath through her open mouth.

Anika anchored her hands on her hips. "What the hell's wrong with you?"

Evan spit out a stream of saliva and blood onto the gel mat. She dragged the back of her hand across her mouth, raised her gaze—her eyes glittered in anger. And something else.

"Mari's dead."

Chapter 20

Darkness swallowed Anika. All around her, inky silence. She couldn't see. Couldn't hear. Couldn't talk. Couldn't feel... anything. It felt good not to feel. Feeling was dangerous. Feeling would destroy her. Better, safer not to feel.

She lay on the couch in her living room, too exhausted to climb the stairs to her bed, and pulled the blanket tighter around her shoulders. She willed her mind to stay blank, residing in a gray state between wakefulness and sleep.

At some point, sleep won out. She realized this when she awoke to the sensation that someone had entered the room. Without opening her eyes, she knew who it was. A tug of connection pulled at her. *Gianni.*

Was he going to say how sorry he was? That he knew how she felt? That he, too, had lost a fellow operative, a friend, in a mission? And he had gotten through this dark time. That she would, too.

She didn't want to hear it.

She rolled away from him, her back a silent command. *Go away.*

"It's been forty-two hours, Anika, since you logged into the agency. Your tracking chip situates you here all that time."

Forty-two hours. It could have been forty-two days for all she knew.

"It's time to come back inside. Run sims. Return to the training facility. Study up on your languages. Memorize safe house locations.

You have to maintain your proficiency levels."

At his choice of words, the dispassion in his voice, a spark of fury shot up Anika's spine, from tailbone to the top of her head. Even though she didn't want his sympathy, his complete lack of feeling infuriated her. She fisted her blanket and jerked back to face him, muscles coiled as if ready to strike. Gianni stood one meter away, a dim shadow in the darkened room.

He was acting so cold. Where was the man who had made champagne-fueled, crazy-hot love to her in this very place only days ago? The man who had left her the intimate message? Where had he gone? Maybe he didn't exist, except in her imagination. Maybe Second was right and Anika had mistaken Gianni's behavior for something it wasn't. Maybe it was just the necessary preparation of a junior agent for a dangerous undercover mission.

Fury burned through her. "That's all you care about? My *proficiency levels?*"

"You have to train as if your life depends on it. Because it does."

"What are you implying? That Mari—" She couldn't say it out loud. *That Mari died.* "That Mari...is responsible for...what happened to her? Because she didn't *train* hard enough?"

"That's not what I'm saying."

"Then what? If Mari wasn't ready, why didn't you stop her from being assigned a mission?"

Anika saw again Mari's face, her big brown eyes radiating fear, before she headed to Transport. Mari had been so scared, despite her final brave words. Guilt stabbed at Anika. *Why didn't I stop her? Why didn't I push her harder on rappelling?*

"Put aside your feelings. Recommit to your training," Gianni said. "Lying here isn't going to bring Mari back."

Anger, guilt, sadness pummeled Anika's insides until she felt numb.

"Meet with Psych. Take meds. Do whatever you need to do," Gianni said.

"I can't do anything. I can't move. I feel..." *Empty, nothing, blank.* Anika collapsed back against the couch, shrunk into the blanket. "I feel...dead...inside." She searched out his gaze, wanted desperately to connect with the man, not the operative. But the dimness of the room prevented her from seeing anything except his shadowy outline. Not even a glint of the pendant he always wore. "Maybe that's what it takes to succeed in U.N.I.T. If so, I should leave—"

"Don't," Gianni said, cutting her off. He took a step closer. Tension vibrated off him. "Don't say it. Don't think it."

"Go away," Anika said, fatigue coating her throat. "Just...go. Please."

"You've been assigned your first interrogation. It's a chance to put your training into practice."

"Haven't you been listening?" She blew out an angry breath. "I can't go back in right now. I just...can't."

"You'll be interrogating the hostile who shot Mari."

"What?" Anika bolted upright. "Mari was *shot*? I thought she fell. She told me the mission required a long rappel." Anika knew Mari shouldn't have told her anything about the mission. It was against orders. But what did that matter now? Mari was dead. "She was so scared before she went out."

Anika had replayed the horrible scene in her mind, over and over. Mari falling backward in space, her slender frame plummeting to the hard ground. Eyes wide, mouth open in a silent scream. Only she hadn't died that way.

"Mari completed the rappel. She was hit after she landed," Gianni said.

So, Mari had conquered her greatest fear, Anika thought. All that additional practice had paid off. Except... she was still dead.

"Her body armor didn't protect her?"

"It did. She had removed her night vision patches. Perhaps they had gotten damaged during the descent. Wardrobe discovered a crack in the right one. The bullet caught her..."

"Oh my God," Anika whispered. The bullet had caught Mari between the eyes, or penetrated one eye, or a cheek. A new horrible scene replaced the one she had been imagining. "How did you capture her killer?"

"We sent out another team. They acquired five targets. One of Mari's team members identified the man who shot her."

Gianni's words lit a small fire inside her, chasing away some of the darkness. "What does U.N.I.T. want from him?"

"The cell's planned attack that Mari's team was sent to disrupt is still active. We need specifics. Day, time, location."

"Why me?" Anika asked.

"As I said, it's part of your training."

Anika wasn't sure she could be trusted in the same room with the man who had killed her friend. What if she lost control and... "I'd like to practice with a sim first."

"There's no time. The attack could be imminent." Gianni paused, as if debating whether to say more. "If you extract the necessary intel, U.N.I.T. will have no further use for the man. He will be terminated. You can request handling it yourself."

Anika's breath caught in her throat. She only had to maintain control long enough to get the man to talk. After that... The fire inside her burned hotter. "What do we know about him? Anything we can use?"

"His name is Mick Ryan. He was recruited into the cell when he was seventeen. His file's been uploaded on your handheld," Gianni said. "Passcode is alpha-tango-seven-three-zero."

As soon as the door clicked shut behind him, she snatched up her handheld, punched in the code, and started reading.

Chapter 21

Anika strode down a corridor that led to the agency's interrogation zone. Her boots hammered against the floor. The deadening despair of the past days was gone. A renewed sense of purpose flowed through her, like a rain-replenished stream after a long drought. She had Gianni to thank for that. Even if she still bristled at his tactics, he had pulled her out of the darkness.

She nodded at the dark-haired, broad-chested guard outside "A" Room, then stepped forward into a room that resembled the one where she had debriefed her last mission. Only this time, she wasn't the one sitting in the hard metal chair. This time, she was the one who'd be asking the questions. And getting answers. Ones that would prevent innocent lives from being destroyed.

Mick Ryan looked older than the picture in his file, which approximated his age as mid-twenties. Anika wondered if spending years in the shadows, under constant threat of being discovered as a member of a terrorist cell, aged a person. He was still attractive, in a boy-next-door way, with reddish brown hair, even features, and an athletic build. His hazel eyes were bloodshot, most likely from lack of sleep. His fair skin, at least the parts not covered by his T-shirt and camo pants, displayed no marks of previous interrogation, though the magnetized shackles around his ankles and wrists would leave bruises. The intel in his file had been thin, mostly full of the anti-everything screeds he had been writing since the age of twelve from his hometown of Boston, Massachusetts. Still, she had something to work with. Or, she would, as soon as the tech-geeks sent her what she had requested before leaving her loft.

Ryan glanced at the tube of water in her hand, then looked away. But not before she caught the flicker of interest in his gaze. "Fuck that," he said. "You think that's going to make me talk? Bring in the bad op, sweetheart. You're wasting my time."

Anika quirked her lips into a smile and held up the tube. "What, this?" She popped open the top. "It's not for you." She forced back a few gulps, even though she wasn't thirsty, then tossed the half-empty container on the floor. A thin stream of the liquid dribbled out, in range of Ryan's vision. He licked his lips and swallowed. "This, however..." she said, drawing out the hand laser from the back of her waistband. "This could be for you. It all depends on how quickly and accurately you answer my questions."

"Like I said, you're wasting my time," Ryan sneered. "Just shoot me and be done with it."

"But you haven't even heard my questions," Anika said.

"What are you doing?" Gianni's voice sounded through her ear comm. He was in the observation room nearby, watching and listening. "Stop stalling. Ask about the planned attack."

She stepped behind Ryan and stared into the camera in the upper corner of the room. She raised her crossed hands, palms up, then lowered them into closed fists. *Trust me*, she signed.

"Proceed," Gianni said.

Anika circled Ryan until she was standing in front of him again. The handheld in her front jacket pocket vibrated. *Finally.* She removed the device and studied the video that had been uploaded only seconds ago. A young boy, about ten years old, rode an airboard down a tree-lined street.

130

"How much do you love your little brother?" She turned the screen so the man could see it. Tapped the replay button. Ryan stiffened, his gaze riveted on the image. "His name's Richard, isn't it?" Anika said. "Ricky, for short. Only you call him 'Sticky Ricky' because he loves taffy." She pulled the handheld away. "Sweet."

Ryan's lips tightened into a thin, mean line. "Fuck you, bitch." His right hand curled into a fist.

"Wrong answer." Anika jammed the barrel of the laser into Ryan's mouth. His eyes goggled. "Let's try again. Different question." She could see the tiny inflamed veins, the flecks of gold around his pupils. "We know your cell is planning another attack. We want the details. Where and when? You tell me that and your little brother will continue to eat taffy. Will continue to attend St. Francis Academy in West Roxbury. Will continue to live." She shoved the laser in deeper until he gagged, then yanked it out and stepped back.

Ryan coughed and sputtered, his chest heaving. When he had regained control, he said, "You're bluffing. You won't hurt him. You people have policies. Rules. You don't kill innocents."

"True," Anika said. "However, that's not how my people would describe your brother."

Ryan's brows formed a question.

"In this particular case, we consider him collateral damage."

Ryan lunged against his restraints. "I'm going to fuck you up."

Anika held her ground. She activated her handheld. "Alpha Team," she spoke into the device, "get ready to grab the boy. On my count." She paused to look at Ryan. "Five seconds." A beat passed. "Four-three-two—"

"I'll tell you," Ryan said. He dropped his head, mumbled a few words. "One. Go—"

"Wait." Ryan's head snapped up, his eyes bulging with fear and fury. He dropped his head back, opened his mouth, and howled, like a trapped animal. When he spoke, his answers were clear and direct.

The agency had twelve hours to avert the attack in a megaplex in downtown Seattle. Anika hoped it would be enough time.

"Stand down, Alpha Team," she said. "Do you copy?"

"Well played," Gianni spoke into her ear comm. "I'll be leading our counterattack team. Second is doing the briefing. I'm headed there now. As soon as the intel is verified, he's yours. Do you copy?"

Anika stared into the camera. The question, unbidden, stole through her mind. *Will you come find me when you get back?*

"Copy that." She slid the handheld back inside her pocket. She wished she hadn't discarded the tube of water. Her mouth felt as dry and hot as the noonday sun in a New Angeles summer. She looked down at Ryan, his frame collapsed against the chair. "We're confirming what you've just told me. Once we do, we'll recall the team on your brother."

"Then what?" he asked. "You'll drop me in some deep dark hole?"

"The only hole you're going into is on the other side of a laser blast. It's called hell."

"You may want to rethink that," he said.

She crossed her arms. "Oh?"

Ryan's eyes softened. A smile tugged at his lips. The combination emanated boyish charm—if that boy hadn't grown up to be a terrorist. One who had killed her friend. "If you keep me on this side of hell, you can arrange to intercept comms from my...colleagues about the next attack. And the one after that."

"We have other colleagues of yours. We don't need you." *You cocky prick.*

"That may be so. But I'm, well...not all my associates are equally informed."

"Don't tell me," Anika said. "You're one of the *masterminds*?"

"Your word, sweetheart, not mine."

"Well, here's a word for you. Three, actually. *Fuck your offer.* My orders are to terminate you. And I've never been so happy to follow orders as I am now."

"Even if it means risking the lives of so many innocents?"

"Innocents?" Anger rose within Anika, a red-hot geyser ready to erupt. She whipped out her handheld and jabbed the screen. The picture of Mari she had taken at the bottom of the rappelling wall stared back at her. Her friend's rosy cheeks and bright eyes vibrated with life. Pain and loss stabbed Anika. She turned the screen to face Ryan. "Her name was Mari. She was my friend. She was also part of the team sent to stop your attack. Trying to prevent innocents from being killed. For God's sake, *she* was an innocent. And you shot her. So I'm going to shoot you." Anika drew out her laser. Set the barrel against Ryan's forehead, between his eyes. "Right here. Like you did to my friend."

Anika longed to follow through on her threat. The urge to pull the trigger was almost overpowering. She wanted to obliterate the look in Ryan's eyes. It seemed like the only way to avenge Mari's death and defuse her own anger. She started to squeeze the trigger.

Ryan's gaze zeroed in on her finger and froze. The color leached from his face.

Doubt snaked through Anika. She worried that killing for vengeance, instead of for protection, would corrupt her. She would cross a moral line that she couldn't step back from. But Ryan couldn't suspect her doubt.

"I can't discharge this laser into your brain until the intel you've given us is confirmed," she said. "Don't worry. It shouldn't be too much longer." She released the trigger and her breath at the same time.

The spark in Ryan's eyes died. His shoulders sagged in defeat.

Anika spun around and stalked out of the room. In the corridor outside, while the mega-sized guard continued to stand watch, she paced. Up and down. Up and down. She clutched her handheld and stared at the dark screen, willing it to activate, impatient for an update from Gianni.

Come on. Confirm the damn intel.

Even as the words repeated themselves in Anika's mind, doubt continued to wind through her. How would killing Ryan resolve anything? It wouldn't bring Mari back. It wouldn't even stop future attacks. While Ryan might know about the attack in Seattle, his boast about being the cell's mastermind was just that. A bullshit boast by a man desperate to save his own skin. If he were the mastermind, U.N.I.T. would keep him alive. Extract as much additional intel as possible. Or hold him for a future trade. No, Mick Ryan wasn't that important. Just a low-level foot soldier in a terrorist network. That was the real reason U.N.I.T. had approved his termination. Anika had been through enough training to know that much.

So, how would her killing him make a difference? Or was this just another part of her advanced training? To learn how to kill on command, no questions asked? To play on her emotions, her feelings over Mari's death, to do the agency's dirty work? This wasn't like the time in the training facility when she had killed to save Mari and stop a terrorist from escaping. This time, she would be killing a man who had already been neutralized, who would never be able to take another innocent's life. But what about Mari?

Anika stopped pacing and leaned against the side wall. She pulled up the image of her friend's face on the handheld. *How can I make it up to you? Is preventing the attack in Seattle, finishing the mission you gave your life for, enough?* Anika returned to home screen and scanned in vain for a message from Gianni. *Where are you?* She couldn't keep pacing here as the questions and doubts continued to chase one another through her mind.

"I'll come back," she told the guard and was awarded a micro-nod of his massive head.

She visited the training facility. The familiar sights, pungent smells, and clamorous sounds were a balm, soothing her agitation. A sense of calm settled over her. *Was this what home felt like?* As a kid growing up in the orphanage, she had always wondered.

She knew where she wanted to spend the remaining wait time. She headed toward the back of the gigantic space, past the different zones where agents practiced running, punching, throwing, shooting. When she reached the rappelling area, she harnessed up and started her ascent. At the end of the third rappel, her handheld buzzed. The screen lit up with the message she had been hoping for. *Intel confirmed. Proceed with termination.*

Anika toweled the sweat from her face. She looked up at the wall that had instilled such fear in Mari. A fear her friend had overcome in order to save innocents. Those innocents were now being saved. Maybe not by Mari, but by the agency that had rescued her from a lifetime of imprisonment. Given her a chance to do something more with her life. Just as it had given Anika.

She continued staring up at the wall until it disappeared from view into the darkness high above. Something settled inside her.

Mari's sacrifice hadn't been in vain. She had died for something she believed in.

But what should Anika do about Ryan? The agency had made the decision about his fate; if she didn't carry out the termination, someone else would. Anika brought up her friend's picture again. *Do you want ME to terminate him? I'll do it, if it's what you want. But I'd rather not.*

Mari's voice whispered through her mind. "Don't." The voice grew louder. "Don't do it." And louder still. "Don't let this place turn you into someone you're not." Anika waited, but nothing more came. It was enough. A calm wave, born of certainty, rolled through her.

She punched the buttons on her handheld and contacted Clinic. After providing her tracking ID number as verification, she said, "There's a patient for you in the interrogation zone, 'A' Room."

"Terminal or viable?" the medic asked.

"Terminal."

Anika's hands and heartbeat were steady as she released the rappelling harness. She had just given an order to kill. Regardless of the euphemism the agency preferred, termination was still killing. No pang of remorse arrowed through her. Or regret. Was that because a part of her had died? Maybe. But the waves of emotions that Gianni's mention of the interrogation had roused in her—surprise, vengeance, anger, determination—told her she had plenty of life left. She wasn't dead inside. She was restored, resolute, and ready to resume her training.

Chapter 22

Gianni did find Anika upon his return from the mission, though not in the way she wanted. At least he had the decency to let her know, via e-message, the mission in Seattle had been a success.

After that, their contact was limited to one-way communications sent to her handheld. Gianni assigned her a list of advanced training tasks: tracking time with breath-counting during extended mission sims; infiltrating multi-secured compounds; dismantling ever more intricate bombs; devising attack plans for hostiles embedded with innocents.

For several days, Anika trained with a commitment and intensity she hadn't felt since her first weeks as a recruit, when she had been terrified of failing. Terrified of being kicked out of U.N.I.T., the one place in her life that had chosen her. A choice that began to heal the deep wound of rejection inflicted by being abandoned by her birth mother and never being adopted.

She turned down invitations from Evan to get together for drinks at Amnesia. Partly because she didn't want alcohol and a late night to interfere with her next day's performance. And partly because she wasn't ready to face Evan and the memory of their last interaction, when the tech ops officer had delivered the devastating news about Mari.

In between her assigned tasks, she spent time in the training facility and honed her physical skills. At the end of each day, she reviewed her scores. Satisfaction, like well-chilled wine, coursed through her when she set new agency records—as did frustration, like wine gone sour, when she didn't.

Never once did Gianni send feedback. No words of praise or encouragement. Or even criticism.

It wasn't at all what she'd expected when he'd told her after her very first mission—their first mission together—that he'd be supervising her advanced training. At the time, she'd thought that meant more time with him. She still remembered the buzz of anticipation that had shot through her when he'd promised to teach her how to pilot a jet plane. They had been standing on the tarmac after the harrowing escape from the North Korean embassy. The custom aircraft had resembled a sleek mechanical bird, outlined in the moonlight. Anika had imagined the two of them together in the small cockpit cruising through an endless sky.

Instead, she was stuck on the ground, with Gianni nowhere to be seen. Maybe it was better this way. Without him around, there were no distractions to pull her focus from becoming a top agent.

Then, two weeks after their return from El Salvador, Gianni showed up. Anika had just finished a long, muscle-relaxing soak when her front door buzzed. Through her security monitor, she studied him. He was dressed casually, in jeans, boots, and a leather jacket, his hair hanging loose around the collar. Slung across one shoulder was a warming pouch. In his hand, he held a bottle of wine.

At first, she was cool toward him. As he crossed the threshold into her loft, she asked in her best neutral voice, "What's in the bag?" She hoped her coolness masked the anger and hurt caused by his distance, his unexplained absence over the past days. And she hoped it masked other emotions—anxiety, doubt—fueled by her trainers' cautions not to get emotionally involved with anyone, including a fellow operative.

And by Second's warning not to confuse Gianni's behavior with real feelings of affection.

"Dinner," Gianni said, unpacking the bag. "*Pollo alla cacciatora.* My mother's special recipe."

The mention of his mother disarmed Anika. Gianni had only mentioned her once before, during their mid-mission dance at the North Korean embassy, while they were pretending to be a couple. He had told Anika she reminded him of his mother, whom he described as intelligent, strong, brave, and protective of others.

A tantalizing aroma of tomatoes, onion, and garlic scented the air. Anika's stomach clamored in response. "It's a good thing I've earned extra food credits from all the training this past week," she said.

"This meal is within your allotment."

"How do you know?" She shot the question at him. So much for trying to remain cool.

"I've been following you." He pulled out a red rose from the pouch and walked over to stand close to her. "The past two weeks." He held out the flower.

"Really? From where?" Anika crossed her arms. "Where have you been?"

"I wish I could tell you." He lowered his hand with the flower still in it. "But you know why I can't." His gaze steadied on her.

Anika huffed out a breath. "A mission. One that I'm not part of. So I can't know about it."

"Yes. I leave again tomorrow. I don't know for how long. I should actually be prepping for it now."

"Then why aren't you?" she demanded.

"Because," Gianni said, "I'd rather spend the time with you." His eyebrows drew together, a hint of concern in his gaze. "If you'll have me."

Anika could feel herself softening toward him. He was choosing *her* over work for a change. He was asking for her understanding, her acceptance. Could she give it?

In the silence of her hesitation, Gianni spoke up. "I know things have been difficult between us lately. I'm sorry for that. I haven't wanted to be gone so much. But I don't control the timing of...my assignment. We can have tonight. If you say so." He held out the flower to her again. "I hope you will."

She took the flower and inhaled its rich scent, a balm to her troubled emotions. "Just dinner."

He smiled, his eyes lighting with pleasure. "As you wish." He finished setting out the food, poured the wine, and proceeded to seduce her all over again.

The food and drink were intoxicating enough. But it was the stories Gianni told of his family that captured her heart. Even while they also made it bleed a little.

Although an only child, Gianni had grown up with grandparents, aunts, uncles, and cousins. Lots and lots of cousins. They gathered often, for weekly meals, birthday parties, holiday celebrations. Get-togethers filled with laughter, tears, shouts, hugs.

With each memory he shared, the lines around Gianni's eyes and mouth softened, the emotional distance between them shortened.

"My cousin, Marco, and I had our first, and last, real fight over a girl," Gianni said. "She was in our same grade at school. We were twelve." He took a sip of wine, his gaze turned toward the past. He lay on floor pillows next to the couch where Anika lounged. Opera music played in the background. "We agreed that the only honorable way to decide who should pursue her was with our fists. Our older cousin refereed."

"Who won?" Anika asked

"I did, of course." Gianni smiled up at her. Its tenderness stole her breath.

"So you got the girl?"

Gianni shook his head. "She was already dating someone else. He was two classes ahead of us. And a foot taller."

"Foolish girl," Anika whispered under her breath.

"If she had been you, I wouldn't have walked away so easily."

Gianni's gaze heated her skin and melted her determination to keep him at arm's length. How could she resist him when he looked at her like that? She glanced away. "It sounds wonderful. To have grown up with such a big family."

"It was," Gianni said.

"Do you get to visit them much now?"

"No, not since..." Gianni's voice trailed off. The lines around his eyes deepened. "Not since joining the agency."

Sadness crept over Anika. "Well, you have your memories."

Gianni sat up and placed his hand over both of hers, which had somehow formed a tight grip in her lap. "There's still time," he said. "For making new memories."

She looked at him, a single tear rolling down her cheek. "Do you really think so?"

"I do." He brushed the tear away.

"Even inside the agency? With its rule against emotional attachments?"

"The rule is a means to an end. Mission proficiency. As long as we perform to the agency's standards, we have some leverage."

She dropped her gaze to their joined hands. So much was at stake for every mission. At the thought, pressure built in her chest making it hard to breathe. "We have to be excellent. Always."

"Yes." Gianni cupped her chin in his hand and lifted it so she would meet his gaze. "With excellence comes advancement, seniority. And privileges. If we're patient."

Looking into his eyes, Anika could almost see it. A path forward. A way to have both Gianni and U.N.I.T. She took in a breath.

"I've thought about agreeing to...the procedure. To prevent a family. Permanently."

Every Level 1 was offered sterilization. The agency presented it as a convenience, even as a safety precaution, especially for female operatives. An unwanted pregnancy would be, at best, a distraction from fieldwork and, at worst, a physical risk during an extended deep cover assignment. There was also an unspoken understanding that agreeing to the medical procedure would signal an operative's strong commitment to the agency. That held appeal for Anika.

For her, it hadn't even seemed like that big of a decision because she had never imagined herself as a mother. She had never gushed, like the girls at the orphanage or at school, when they talked about their plans for having babies. She didn't get all gooey over images of women who were pregnant, or pushing strollers, or holding the hands of wobbly toddlers. She knew nothing about motherhood, except for its absence. That didn't seem like a good foundation for bringing a child into this world. Still, she hadn't gone ahead with the medical procedure. She wasn't entirely sure why. Maybe the man in front of her had had something to do with her decision to hold onto that part of herself.

"Don't agree to it." Gianni squeezed her hands. "Promise me."

The pleading look in his eyes was something she hadn't seen before. It crumbled her resolve to resist him. And strengthened her resolve to stay open to the possibility of a newly-imagined future. "I promise."

She wanted him to lean forward and kiss her. Craved his lips against hers.

Instead, he removed his hand and stood. "Well," he said, "I know it's getting late." He turned away and started packing up.

Late? Anika was revved, as if her skin had absorbed a dozen WideAwake strips.

When she realized he intended to follow her directive about leaving after dinner, she stopped him with an outstretched hand and the only words that came to mind. "I'm thinking...dessert." A fiery river of desire raced through her.

Gianni's lips across her fingertips fed oxygen to the flames. "I didn't bring any."

"I did." Anika stood. "Upstairs."

Gianni smiled, then gestured toward the staircase. "After you."

Chapter 23

"To Mari." Anika clinked Evan's glass and tossed back a shot of whiskey. The icy liquid refreshed her like a deep dive into a plunge pool.

Evan refilled their glasses from the bottle on the table. Her head bobbed to the thrumming beat from Amnesia's sound system. They sat near the dance floor and watched bodies undulate to the techno-world music. "Want to dance?"

"Maybe later." Anika ran her finger around the rim of her glass, but didn't pick it up. The whiskey was already making her head feel fuzzy and her limbs boneless. The rigorous training and strict diet from the previous week had lowered her tolerance for alcohol. Still, she was glad she was here. She had been the one to suggest to Evan they meet up.

"Do you think Mari appreciates our tribute?" Anika smoothed her hand over the wig she had borrowed from Wardrobe. Both she and Evan wore the same style, cut and shaped like their friend's newly-shorn hair, before she had gone out on her fateful, final mission. The contact lenses in their eyes matched Mari's robin's-egg-blue color. They had even painted a sprinkling of freckles across their noses and cheeks to add to the likeness.

"I think she's laughing her ass off," Evan replied. She was already two shots ahead of Anika. "To you." She touched her glass to Anika's still full one. "You've earned it."

Anika tipped back the contents in one smooth turn of her wrist. She *had* earned it. And she deserved a break from her grueling training regimen. After all, no list of new tasks from Gianni awaited her. In fact, she hadn't had any more communication from him since their night together. He had disappeared again.

For weeks, she hadn't seen him in the agency's corridors, inside or outside briefing rooms, or in the training facility. Different trainers, each with a particular specialty, supervised her now. Evan had conducted today's series of challenges. After Anika had completed the final one—hacking into a fake military security system with next-gen AEG encryption—she had offered to buy Evan a drink.

"Thanks for coming out," Anika said. "What happened to Mari...I'm sure it hasn't been easy on you, either."

"I'm so glad that bastard..." Evan trailed off as she cast a glance around the room pulsing with light and sound. She set a palm-sized object on the small table between them. With its iridescent material, it looked as innocuous as a woman's mini-clutch. "There. Now we can talk."

"What is that?" Anika asked.

"I call it 'Hush.'"

"What's it do?"

"Blocks sound within a one-meter radius. My latest invention."

"The name doesn't sound very tech."

"When *you* can invent a gadget that prevents anyone from listening to your conversation, you can call it whatever you want."

"Point made," Anika said.

"As I was saying, I'm delighted the bastard who killed Mari was terminated," Evan said. "It's a good thing he wasn't valuable enough to keep alive. I only wish I could have been the one to terminate him."

Anika avoided Evan's gaze. How would Evan feel if she knew Anika could have been the one to do the termination, but decided against it?

Would she consider it a betrayal of Mari?

"That guy on the dance floor looks like he fancies you," Evan said after a moment.

Anika's head swiveled. "What guy?" For a crazy moment, she thought she might see Gianni, even though she had never seen him in here. Not even when he *had* come that one time—the last time she, Evan, and Mari had been together. It seemed ages ago now.

A dark-haired, medium-built man was, indeed, staring at her. His head turned continually in her direction, even as his body swiveled and snaked against another woman on the dance floor.

Definitely not Gianni. She looked away. Disappointment deflated her, like a child's popped balloon. "Not interested."

"Why not? He looks like he could be good for a quick shag."

Anika shook her head and took another sip.

"I mean," Evan continued, "I know he's not as cool-hot as Brambilla." Anika choked on the liquid. "But then, who is? That man is definitely shag material. Best enjoyed slow and low, am I right?"

"I don't..." Whiskey burned in Anika's windpipe. She wiped the back of her hand across her mouth. "How would I know?"

"Come on." Evan tapped the scrambler. "It's just the two of us."

"Really. There's nothing to share. You know the agency doesn't approve of relationships."

"The agency doesn't have to know everything about everything," Evan said.

"What makes you think there's anything to know?"

"Hmmm." Evan's eyes narrowed.

Anika forced herself to sit still and meet her friend's gaze.

"I watched the replay of your first mission," Evan said after an extended pause. "The North Korean embassy gala."

"And?" Anika's mind flashed back to the most searing memory from that night. Their first kiss. But it had happened in the protective shadow of the jet plane, out of sight of the other U.N.I.T. agents. Surely, they hadn't been seen on camera.

"There was a moment between you on the dance floor. The way he held you, a look that passed between you. I mean," Evan said, rolling her eyes, "I know you were only meant to be playing the part of a couple, but I find it hard to believe you're both that good as actors."

Anika wondered if that moment was when Gianni had said she reminded him of his mother. When he had kissed her hand and told her she was beautiful.

She needed to change this topic of conversation. Fast. She didn't trust Evan, or anyone, to know that Gianni's and her relationship was anything other than professional. It was too great a risk to her future with the agency.

"I could have been the one to do it. Terminate Ryan," she said. "I was given permission."

"What do you mean, 'could have been'?"

"I thought I would go through with it. As soon as the intel about the mission was validated. It's what got me off my couch, out of my apartment. The promise of avenging Mari. But in the end," Anika said, shaking her head, "I called Clinic to take care of it."

"Why?" Evan gripped her glass until her knuckles bulged.

"What good would it do?" Anika shrugged one shoulder. "It wouldn't change anything. Wouldn't bring Mari back."

"If it had been me," Evan said, downing another shot, "I wouldn't have hesitated to laser blast his ass to hell."

"How do you know? Have you ever killed someone?"

"How do you think I ended up as a lifer in Bronzefield Prison?" Evan said. "I mean, I didn't *know* for sure people were going to die when I blew up the House of Lords. But it was the middle of a weekday. So it was a safe bet that not everyone would survive."

"That was *you*?" Anika asked. She remembered the nonstop media coverage. The undisclosed identity of the underage perpetrator.

Evan nodded.

"What...happened?"

"I was angry at the world." Evan stared into her empty glass. "And my mum and dad. Both diplomats. More interested in jaunting around the globe to negotiate peace than spending time with me."

The hurt in Evan's voice echoed through Anika. She thought about how unwanted she had felt growing up in a federal orphanage. She had always believed a home, any home, would be better than that. But maybe not.

Evan's lips twisted. "There was a boy in my little group. Thought he was better than everybody. A real square, but good-looking. The wanker didn't think I could hack into the building's antiterrorist system and reverse-activate it."

"I don't understand," Anika said.

"The system was programmed to repel a terrorist attack. I reprogrammed it to self-detonate." Evan's lips tightened. "Guess I bloody showed him. And them." She looked up. "Do you think I'm a monster?"

"No." Anika shook her head. *Only a hurt, angry little girl seeking attention. One with prodigious tech skills. Tragic for the people working in the House of Lords that day. Fortunate, now, for U.N.I.T.* "And now you get to use your amazing talents to fight the bad guys. You're making up for...the past."

"I don't know about that. But, at least now, I'm not spending my days and nights in a mega-security prison. What's your excuse for joining the agency?"

"Oh, you know, making the world safe. Being part of something bigger than myself. Blah, blah." Anika couldn't bring herself to talk about the many rejections in her own past. How they created a deep longing within her. To be chosen, to feel special. Time for another topic change. "Well, back to Ryan. All I know is, I couldn't do it."

"You do realize 'wet work' is a key requirement of the agency, right?"

"Of course. When it's necessary to save lives."

"As decided by the higher ups. They order. We obey. Or else."

"Not blind obedience. I didn't sign up for that."

"You signed the contract when you were recruited, didn't you? Did you read it? Because I don't recall it including an opt-out clause if you don't agree with an order."

Anika remembered signing a lot of documents for the recruiter. Medical, psychological, financial, academic, social. They were full of legal terms she didn't understand. At the time, what she understood was that she had been singled out among all the other kids who had never been adopted. She had finally been chosen. When the federal orphanage was preparing, in their words, "to transition her to independence" (in her words, "to kick her out") because she had aged out of the system, she had been given a lifeline by an agency called U.N.I.T. But now that lifeline was starting to feel like a chokehold.

"If that's what it takes to succeed, maybe I should leave." She shoved her chair back from the table. It was the second time she had spoken it out loud. First, with Gianni, when he had come to her loft to tell her about Ryan's capture. And now. "Maybe I'm not cut out for it." The air around her was thick with sweat and alcohol. Her head buzzed like a pissed-off hornet. She gulped in a breath.

Time to call it a night.

"Oh, you're perfectly suited to it." Evan refilled their glasses.

Something in Evan's tone siren-blared through Anika. "What makes you so sure?"

Evan glanced at the scrambler and motioned Anika forward, within the device's range. "Because you passed their tests with flying colors."

Chapter 24

"You mean the pre-recruit qualifying exams?" Anika asked, sitting back down.

Evan snorted. "I mean the exams you took while growing up. From baby school all the way through secondary school. You remember? Four-dimensional thinking, creative problem solving, observational skills, facial and emotional recognition, role playing, physical endurance, and on and on. All supervised by the orphanage."

"Are you talking about game day?" Anika remembered the monthly Saturdays, attended only by federal orphans, in the school's basement. Even the room's stale smell and harsh lights couldn't lessen the excitement tingling through her, especially when she won in her age group and advanced to a higher level. Game day had been the highlight of each month. Even better than the smoke ring contests she won against the boys in the orphanage.

"Game day. Is that what they called it?" Evan said. "More precisely, 'evaluation day.'" The agency was monitoring and evaluating you. Well, not *just* you. Everyone who performed well. Scouting their future agents. I thought you knew." Her brows furrowed. "Oh, that's right, I forgot. You're only a Level One. The way you handled the crap I threw at you today, you're primed for Level Two. Is it hot in here?" She blew out a breath. "I'm feeling a bit...hot."

"Wait, go back." Anika's hand gripped the edge of the table to ground herself in a world about to tilt and shake. "Future agents? What are you talking about? The games were held at the school. They were a special activity for federal orphans only."

"I need to use the loo."

Anika's hand shot out and grabbed Evan's wrist. "How could U.N.I.T. know what was going on at the school?"

Evan looked down at her wrist. "Ow," she said, blinking. "You don't have to come with me. I can manage."

Anika slammed her hand down, still holding onto Evan, against the table. "Tell me."

Evan's head bobbed up. Her gaze drifted over Anika, then settled, focused. "U.N.I.T. has two recruiting pools. Life row in prisons and federal orphanages."

"Yeah, so?"

"So, they monitor both. Constantly searching for promising candidates."

Anika's stomach snarled into knots. "How do you know that?"

"Because," Evan said, sighing with impatience, "I'm a tech goddess. When Command and Second are doing initial evals of the inmates and, you know, the kids, I feed them the files from the prisons and the orphanages. Now, either walk with me to the loo or let go of my wrist."

"One more thing." Anika leaned forward. "Kids like me, who did well in the games—I mean the tests—early on... What if we...if I...had been adopted? How would the agency be able to continue testing and evaluating me?" Her mind fired with possibilities, unwilling to land on the only answer that made sense. "It doesn't seem very efficient. Unless..." The answer exploded in her brain.

Evan squirmed in her seat.

Anika let go of Evan's wrist and slumped back in her seat. "Unless the agency made sure I stayed at the orphanage. Made sure I was never adopted." Her gaze drilled into Evan. The knots in her stomach moved into her chest, stealing her breath. "Is that what they do?"

"Look," Evan said. "Personally, I think recruiting kids from orphanages is rubbish. But I don't make the rules. I just—"

"Obey," Anika said. "Yeah, I get it." She emptied her glass and hoped the whiskey wouldn't come back up as fast as it went down. "I'm out. Want me to order another bottle?"

"That'd be brilliant." Evan stood, swayed, steadied. "Now, if you'll excuse me."

As she passed by, Anika reached out a hand. "Does Gianni know? About keeping kids in orphanages in order to recruit them later on?"

"I've no idea." Evan shrugged. "He might. You could always ask him. The way he checks up on you and monitors your daily performance reports, I imagine you could get away with asking him anything." She gave a lopsided grin. "He was settling into his new office when I left. He's just been promoted to Level Four."

"You saw him?"

"I set up the new passcode for him. Sub-level Two." Evan stood, steadied herself. "Be right back."

Anika tapped in an order for more whiskey on the table's e-pad, paid the tab, and grabbed a complimentary packet of Dry Out.

She gazed toward the dance floor. But instead of the writhing bodies, all she saw was a little girl, with short dark hair and bright blue eyes, in the school's grungy basement, playing—and winning—game day, month after month, year after year.

Chapter 25

"Did you know about the games? How they were used to evaluate me, to recruit me?" *To keep me from having a family of my own?*

Anika stood in front of Gianni's desk where he sat in his new office. Bare walls. A lone monitor on the side console. A chair she had pushed aside.

She held up the device she had taken from Amnesia. "This will allow us to talk privately. It blocks sound within one meter. The new head of tech ops invented it." The cherry aftertaste of Dry Out lingered on her tongue. The sobering liquid had taken effect—her head was clear, but her body was coiled.

"How do you know it works?" Gianni asked, eyeing the shiny object.

"Honestly, I don't care if it does or not." She dropped it on the desktop. "Did you know? Answer me."

He tapped a few buttons on his handheld. The monitor flickered and darkened. "Yes."

She sucked in a quick breath. She had expected a more evasive answer. Or one that recited the agency's policies against revealing information above her clearance level.

"I joined U.N.I.T. because I believed it was the first place that ever thought I was special. That they chose me."

"You are special. And you were chosen," Gianni said.

"I was *targeted*." Anika stabbed her finger into the air. "Because of my skills, my abilities. And only if I maintain my proficiency levels. Isn't that what you said?"

"Why don't you sit?" he asked.

"Because I'm leaving." She spun on her heel and pulled off the wig she had been wearing in Mari's honor. "Because I'm done." She approached the door. *Click.* She yanked on the handle. It didn't budge. Without turning around, she said, "Let me out." She ground her teeth. "I swear to God, if you don't unlock this door..." Fury boiled inside her. *What will I do? How will I make him?* Her hands curled into fists. She wanted to pound the metal surface until the heat was gone. Until all the emotions were gone. Anger, betrayal, hurt. Until there was nothing left inside.

"What if I were a hostile? How would you get me to unlock the door?"

"I'm done performing," Anika said. "Done playing your stupid games. Done with everyone's games. Just let me go."

"Where will you go?"

I have no idea. "Far away from here."

"How will you disable your tracking chip?"

"Every recruit knows how to do that."

"That's a temporary solve. You'll need something permanent. Along with a new ID. Money. Comms. Weapons. Transport. You have them?"

No. "I'll get them."

"You need to secure them *before* you go on the run. And it wouldn't hurt to have at least one contact who can help, preferably someone who owes you a favor. Even then, to my knowledge, no one's ever succeeded."

Anika turned her head. Gianni's gaze was focused on a distant point over her shoulder. "You've thought about it," she said.

He picked up the sound-blocking device, studied it, set it back down. "Convince me to unlock the door."

A tiny flame of hope lit inside Anika. "Come with me." She stepped toward him. "We could go together."

"Why would I do that?"

She rocked back on her heels, his words like water dousing the flame. But then she remembered other words he had said to her. It was time to learn which words he really meant.

"Because of what you said to me at the end of our first mission. And, again, in the training facility, after I shot the hostile. About wanting a relationship. Even though you know it's dangerous. That the agency won't allow it. Not long term."

"The agency can't prevent it as long as we both do what's asked of us."

"What's asked of us," Anika said, repeating his words. "You mean, killing people."

"Hunting terrorists to protect innocents. Like our mission in El Salvador. You don't believe in that?"

"*I'm* an innocent. The agency kept me from ever having a family of my own. Recruited me under false pretenses. I can't accept that."

"Well, I wasn't recruited like you. I was in prison. I knew what I was signing up for."

"Why *were* you in prison? You've said you were responsible for the deaths of four judges, but you never told me the full story."

From underneath his shirt collar, Gianni pulled out the oval medal hanging from the chain around his neck.

Anika remembered him telling her it was all he had left from his family. She could see a raised image on the medal's surface, but didn't know what it represented.

Gianni rubbed a finger along the medal's edge, lost in memory. "My parents were fervent Catholics and social justice revolutionaries. They believed equally in honoring God and in overturning the Italian government which they deemed corrupt and oppressive. They raised me to share their beliefs. I grew up attending masses and protests in equal measure. My parents did not use violence. That didn't stop the government from treating them as if they did. I was sent to live with distant cousins in a different part of Italy, while my parents went into hiding. But they wouldn't stop practicing their faith. The police ambushed them as they left a small church in the countryside after early morning mass. They were both killed. I was thirteen."

Sympathy cooled Anika's anger. *So young,* she thought. *Only a boy.*

"I carried on my parents' work by joining a national resistance movement," Gianni said. "It *was* violent. We destroyed cars, boats, houses, buildings."

"Not people?" she asked, though she knew there had been at least four.

"Not until two years later, when I plotted the bombing of the Italian parliament building. I didn't know there would be people—judges—inside. It was supposed to be empty." Gianni wrapped his fingers around the medal. "I was wrong."

"The medal belonged to your father?"

Gianni nodded. "My mother gave it to him. I removed it from his body at the morgue and placed it around my neck. There was a nick on one edge that hadn't been there. I assume it happened during the attack." He dropped the medal. "Apart from when I have to remove it for a mission, it's with me all the time."

Pinpricks of envy jabbed at Anika's heart. She longed for something tangible from her family. "What does the image mean?"

"It's St. Jude. He's the patron saint of lost causes." A smile ghosted around Gianni's lips. "My parents appreciated irony." He glanced at Anika, sadness radiating from his brown eyes. "Now you know how I ended up in an Italian prison."

She wanted to reach out a hand to offer comfort. "Okay, but you didn't know the judges were inside. You didn't mean to kill anyone. And you were, what, fifteen? You shouldn't have been given a life sentence."

Gianni shrugged. "The Italian courts disagree with you. I was sentenced to live out the rest of my life in a cage—and I would have, if U.N.I.T. hadn't given me back my freedom."

"You think this is freedom?" Anika gestured at the walls around them. "On call twenty-four-seven. Every move monitored. Every thought analyzed. Every mission a life-or-death gamble. You've just traded one prison for another. It doesn't have to be this way."

"For me, it does. For now, anyway." Gianni stood. "I commend your approach."

Click.

Anika pivoted toward the sound. The door swung open. She glanced back at Gianni. "What are you talking about?"

"Trying to convince me that we have a shared enemy. U.N.I.T. It's often an effective tactic when negotiating with a hostile. You're free to go."

Chapter 26

Free. *You're free.* The words whispered through Anika's mind, a seductive siren call.

But for how long?

Gianni was right. She had no plan, no provisions. Anger still simmered inside her, nudging her forward. But uncertainty rooted her in place. That, and something else. Longing. For what could have been. What might still be.

She turned toward him. "Convince me to stay."

"Stay so you can avoid capture. And exile. Stay so you can live."

"Not good enough. Not for me."

Gianni stared at the scrambler still lying on the desk. The muscle at his jaw flexed. He gazed at her, his brown eyes clear, unshadowed. "Then stay for us."

"Us?" Anika's eyes widened. "Ever since you returned from whatever mission you were assigned after the North Korean embassy, you've been...distant. Absent, even. Except, of course, when you were *prepping* me for the mission in El Salvador." Her fists clenched at the memory of Second's warning at the end of her debriefing. "Second advised me not to read too much into your pre-op behavior."

"What did she say?" Gianni's gaze burned into her, through her.

Anika sucked in a breath. "She told me your...actions...were guided by a desire..." *No! Not that word.* "I mean, they were guided by the mission's *objective.* She said I shouldn't interpret them as anything more..." Embarrassment painted her cheeks red. "...more than that." She dropped her gaze.

"Second was wrong."

"She found the message you left for me."

"I told you to delete it."

Anika dipped her head lower. "I know."

"What about the night when I brought dinner and you invited me to stay for...dessert?" A smile teased Gianni's lips. "There was no mission being planned then. That was just about us."

Anika shifted from foot to foot. She remembered that night. Had relived it many nights since. "That was one night. Versus dozens of nights, even weeks, when I had no idea where you were, when you were coming back. *If* you were coming back. Where have you been?"

Gianni sat back down. He tented his fingers, pressed them to his lips as if debating whether to release the answers. "You know it's against agency policy to discuss missions with anyone other than assigned team members?"

"Yes."

"Then you understand what I'm about to tell you is forbidden." His voice was low, grave. He shifted in his seat, once. Then he leaned forward and rested his forearms on the desk. "But it's important to me that you know. This one time. Important for us." His fingers were so tightly linked Anika could see a whitening of his knuckles.

His rare display of nerves elicited a corresponding response in her. The muscles in her shoulders tensed. *It's okay,* she wanted to reassure him. *You can tell me anything.* She stood in place, undecided.

She wanted to know his secrets. But she also wanted to protect him from the agency's censure. In the end, her need to know won out. "I'm listening."

"Are you familiar with 'sweetheart' missions?" he asked.

She nodded. "We learned about them in training. It's when you're assigned a mark to seduce in order to get whatever the agency wants. Intel, an asset, or infiltration of a hostile organization."

"In my case," he said, "it was infiltration. A family-based organization in Eastern Europe acquiring and selling the usual—weapons, drugs, synthetics, military and industrial intel."

"What was your objective?"

"Come sit." Gianni gestured to the chair opposite him. When Anika had settled in, he continued. "My mark was the youngest sister of the man at the top. I used her to get close to him. Gather enough evidence so the regional authorities could take the necessary action."

"And you were successful?"

Gianni nodded.

His silent acknowledgment was a jab to her heart, a painful surprise. Success meant he had slept with the woman. She had thought he could tell her anything, but this was excruciating to hear. She thought back to the moment on the balcony in El Salvador when she had thought (wrongly, as it turned out) that Gianni had slept with Suzette. It had helped to remind her then that it was Gianni's alias, Nino Bianchi, who had done so. Would that same trick work now?

Gianni was staring into the distance, his gaze clouded with an image or a memory only he knew.

Anika decided it was worth trying. "What was your alias on this mission?"

Her question brought Gianni's attention back. "What?" he asked.

"Your *alias*. What was it?"

"Michael Taveggia."

"And the woman's name? The one you...I mean, Michael Taveggia seduced?"

"Sonia Yvanov."

"Michael Taveggia slept with Sonia Yvanov."

"Yes."

Michael slept with her. Michael slept with her. Michael slept with her.

"Did you...have feelings for her?"

"Michael Taveggia did."

"What about Gianni Brambilla?"

Gianni leaned toward her across the desk, palms raised. "My feelings, those feelings, are for you alone."

With his words, his gesture, the throbbing in her heart quieted. He had only done what the mission demanded of him. "What happened to Sonia?"

"She died in the raid by the authorities."

"Another innocent," Anika whispered.

"No. She knew about the family business." Gianni's voice was granite. "Still, she died because she believed the lies I told her. The mission objective was worthy, but it wasn't easy to carry out."

That explained the shadows in his eyes when she had seen him in the training facility. "And that's why you've been so distant with me?"

"I couldn't be with you as I wanted while I was pretending to be in love with someone else. Do you understand?"

Anika nodded. "I want to. I'm trying. What if...you get assigned another sweetheart mission?" *What if I do?* The thought chilled her.

"I have to carry out my assignments, Anika. I made a commitment to U.N.I.T. Second told me I need to do a better job compartmentalizing. I'm working on it."

"U.N.I.T. can make our relationship so hard on us, we'll want to end it," she realized aloud.

"I'm not sure that's possible." Gianni's gaze was so open and direct. There were no shadows now between them. His words breathed hope into her. Could she trust it?

Her gaze dropped to the scrambler still lying on the desk. "I sure hope

Evan's device works."

"I do as well. At that size, it could be very useful in the field. But just in case," Gianni said, gesturing at his handheld, "I activated a privacy function after you arrived. It shields this room but there's a time limit. We have fifty-three seconds left."

"So, what now?" Anika asked. "I continue with my advanced training? How much longer?"

"You still need to learn to fly a plane, remember?"

"You promised to teach me, remember?" *What else do you remember from that night—the moonlit sky, the autumn night breeze, our first kiss?*

"I remember everything, *cara*," Gianni whispered. His tender endearment, his warm gaze told her his memories of that night were as vivid as hers. "I also remember asking you to join me for coffee."

"At the café near here," Anika said, nodding. "You said it reminds you of the one from your home in Brea, Italy."

"We could go there now."

"I don't think it's open. It's past midnight."

"I mean the one in Brea." Gianni's eyes lit up. "We can take a plane. You can have your first lesson."

Anika's brows rose. "You mean tonight? Now?"

Twenty-two seconds.

"We'd arrive at the café as its doors are opening. The perfect time."

Anika sat and considered his invitation. *A real date.* Excitement hummed through her. *One that could be explained away as a training lesson, if anyone ever asked.* The realization that they might always need that kind of professional explanation for being seen together sunk in, tamping down her excitement. Then she leaned into it. If that's what it would take to have both Gianni *and* a place to belong, she would accept it. For the time being. "I like my cappuccino dry, with one sugar and a light dusting of cocoa powder."

Gianni's lips stretched across his face, the smile reaching all the way to his gorgeous brown eyes. "I'll mention that to the server."

Anika took in a breath and nodded. "Okay."

He pressed a button on his handheld. "Transport, this is Brambilla. I need a plane readied for immediate takeoff." He returned his gaze to her. "Okay...does that mean you'll stay?"

She knew he was talking about U.N.I.T now.

Nine seconds.

Anika bit down on her lip. "I can't say for how long."

"But for now?" He held out his hand to her. Not a question from her superior. A supplication from her lover.

"For now..." She took his hand, warm and vibrant, in hers. *One second.* "Yes."

About the Author

Ever since she was a kid playing "spy" with her older sisters, PM Kavanaugh has loved a potent mix of intrigue, danger, and adventure. Now a writer of thrillers spiked with romance, she lives in the Bay Area, California with her clever-enough-to-be-a-spy husband and their aptly named rescue cat, Dash.

You can connect with me on:

🌐 https://www.pmkavanaugh.com
📘 https://www.facebook.com/PMKavanaughWriter
🔗 https://www.instagram.com/pmkavanaughwriter

Also by PM Kavanaugh

Thank you for reading *Dead Inside.* I hope you loved it! The story continues with the third book in the series, *Dead Run.* And if you missed the first book, *Dead Zero*, see below for a sneak peek.

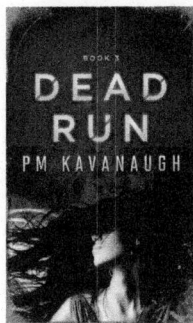

Dead Run

Anika Washington wants out! She's fed up with the agency. And she's led to believe her fellow operative and lover, Gianni Brambilla, has betrayed her. But it's not that simple to leave the agency that owns her. So she fakes her death and runs. Too late, she learns she was deceived about Gianni. And realizes her break for freedom has endangered his life. She battles time, former enemies, and the agency itself to stay alive and save the man she loves.

Available at Amazon and many other digital stores.

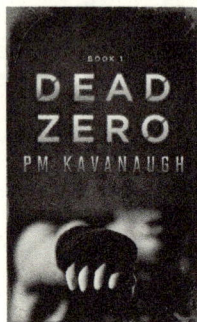

Dead Zero

Dead zero: A recruit that doesn't survive their first mission. Anika Washington is training hard to avoid that fate. Even more, she's determined to excel. Growing up an orphan taught Anika she was never good enough. She will prove them all wrong, including Gianni Brambilla, the senior operative who's taken a special interest in her. Going undercover at a black-tie gala, the pair will need to rely on quick thinking, high-tech spy gadgets, and each other to ensure her first mission's success, or else.

Available at Amazon and many other digital stores.

Made in the USA
Las Vegas, NV
05 February 2022

43137479R10100